The Chinese Jar

Cover illustration: Patrick Arrasmith
Layout & initial caps design: Amy Fortunato
Production: The Actualizers, New York
Printer: Brilliant Graphics

ISBN 978-0-9863541-0-6

This book is typeset in Paperback.

THE
Chinese Jar

Richard A. Pegg

AND

Ann P. Biddle

ACKNOWLEDGEMENTS

We would like to thank our parents.

To all of my many mentors and teachers as well as my wife Ellen and daughter Lily, thank you. RAP

To my family. I am so lucky, words fail me. And to my big brother who kept us going. APB

I would like to thank everyone who helped with the production of this book; from The Actualizers, Amie Cooper and Mikki Kalar with whom collaboration is a constant joy; Amy Fortunato, for her beautiful design, most especially the elegant initial caps for each chapter; Patrick Arrasmith, for his fantastic original cover art; Amanda Davidson, for her editorial acumen; and our printer Brilliant Graphics. RAP

"Andy, I have a jar I want you to look at," said Itchy Carmichael, proprietor of Carmichael's Medieval Arts. Andy had dropped in that morning at the Ocean Terminal shop, on the Kowloon side of Hong Kong harbor, on his way to pick up several handmade shirts. Like most everyone in Hong Kong, Andy's shirts were handmade. "I'm really not a pot person," Andy demurred.

"It's old, it's Chinese, how hard can it be?" asked Itchy.

Andy smiled. He had met Itchy about a year ago. Itchy was an antique dealer specializing in medieval European art and furniture. In fact, he was the only antique dealer of note of medieval European furniture in Hong Kong. Not many collectors of medieval furniture shopped in Hong Kong, but when they did, Itchy was the guy to see.

Itchy had worked hard for his success; he was not a natural fit in the rarefied world of top antique dealers, who were generally smooth, polished, and connected. Nor was Itchy a natural fit in the Hong Kong antiques world, where he had created a niche for medieval European furniture. He was a large man, with dark curly hair and a beard—a small one, but still, it was a rarity in Hong Kong.

It wasn't as though Andy looked native either. He had Itchy's height but only half his bulk. And while Itchy was swarthy, Andy was fair, with dark blond hair and changeable blue eyes. They both blended, though, in Hong Kong's multi-ethnic crowds, feeling right at home.

Andy often cruised the large shopping center, replete with antique shops, souvenir shops, and several tailors, including his own. Once, a year earlier, he'd noticed a large red lacquer travel chest in the window of Itchy's store. Intrigued by the Japanese chest, Andy went in and quizzed Itchy about provenance and price.

The chest had come from an estate sale outside London, thrown in with several other pieces Itchy had purchased. Itchy didn't know what it was, but as any good dealer would tell you, it spoke to him. As with many objects long in museum storage or in someone's attic, it only took the right eyes to recognize an object's provenance. Itchy soon realized that this American lad had those eyes.

Andy saw right away that it was Japanese. It was the right size and configuration for a travel chest, at thirty-eight inches high and fifty inches wide, with no legs or ornate exterior hardware. Andy offered to trace who had commissioned the chest and who'd made it, which would increase its value as much as ten-fold.

The chest itself was rich with clues. The extensive use of gold, black, and red lacquer plus its ornate decorative style suggested the Shibayama family of lacquerers. These artists did their best work during the eighteenth century, and the gold lacquer signature on the interior left door confirmed it was one of theirs. That was the easier task. Next, Andy examined it for clues as to who had commissioned it. On the drawers inside, Andy found depictions of swords and armor and, best yet, a helmet that depicted a family crest. The military equipment suggested a person in the military, and the quality of the piece hinted that it was for a person of high rank. Andy copied down the family crest, or *mon*, then researched samurai families by their crest. He traced the *mon* to a high-ranking samurai named Hosogawa Shigekata, who lived during the eighteenth century. Shigekata was descended from an important daimyo family with several hundred years of pedigree, adding to the chest's cachet. Even without the provenance, it was a valuable piece because of its excellent condition. Most military travel chests showed all too well the hardships of military campaigns, but this one was unusual for its lovely condition. All told, the piece was ten times more valuable than Itchy had surmised, and the two of them sold it to an American museum for 100,000 dollars US. Andy collected twenty percent of the sale price.

The early success pleased them both, but they had more in common than just the sale, and over the past year, a closer friendship had developed. Andy and Itchy were both expatriate Americans, New Yorkers even, living in Hong Kong and working in the art world. When Andy visited Itchy, he also heard the sounds of a home he was nostalgic for, though only at the safe distance of eight thousand miles.

Now, hearing Itchy's Brooklyn tones prompted Andy to inquire, "By the way, I never asked you, but how did you end up in Hong Kong anyway? I mean, what's a nice Jewish boy from Brooklyn doing here?"

"I'm a wandering Jew," Itchy said. "Anyway, they got the best Chinese food on earth here."

"Ever try China?"

"No one there understands a word I say. At least here, after a century of British rule, I have a chance of getting by when ordering food. Even so, people barely understand my name. It's Yitzy, short for Yishmael, but everyone hears 'Itchy.' Some things aren't worth fighting," Itchy shrugged.

Andy laughed. "Okay, show me the pot."

Itchy paused on his walk to the back of the store, which was a wide rectangle with an alcove in the back. "I only have photographs, taken with an instant camera by the owner."

He scooped the photos off his desk and handed them to Andy. They showed a large jar—maybe two feet tall and almost as wide through the shoulders as the base—plus a lid. Andy noted good proportions, a sturdy base that gradually swelled to the shoulders, then a sharper angle from the shoulder to the neck— a classic shape. And the lid looked pretty good. After a moment, Itchy demanded, "Well, what is it?"

Nonplussed, Andy said, "It's a jar."

"The Boy Wonder, you are."

"It's not medieval European, like it says on the front of your shop."

"Nope."

"Mmmmm. Why you?"

"No idea. Maybe he saw the vases in the shop and figured I sold this kind of thing."

Andy glanced at the vases, big colorful examples of recent mass production circa last year, many filled with flowers. It didn't necessarily matter why the seller chose Itchy—many art deals were informally negotiated, to say the least.

"Does your wife still add the flowers every week?"

"Yah. She thinks my stock is too dark and off-putting, so she adds flowers to warm it up."

Andy looked at the pictures again, his face revealing nothing. "Well, it's always difficult to assess an object accurately from a photograph, especially a couple of Polaroids. The color could be way off."

Itchy could not read Andy's face. Andy never revealed what he was thinking—the foreigner with the inscrutable face. He had learned this face from his martial arts teacher, his Sifu. It unnerved people because it was often accompanied by silence. He could see Itchy start to feel uncomfortable.

"It's a Chinese jar," he volunteered. "The decoration and the shape are not Japanese or Korean. The dense decoration, the shape, and the color all are characteristic of the imperial kilns of the fourteenth century. But it could be eighteenth century as well. The Qianlong emperor in the eighteenth century was keen on making copies of earlier pots. He ruled for sixty years, from 1736 to 1796, and he was a great patron of the arts. It could also be a nineteenth century copy, or even a modern knock-off."

Andy paused, considering the jar. "I need to see the color better. The flash typically distorts the colors and they are not distinct here. It's most likely blue and white, because most jars like this are blue and white, but the quality of the cobalt blue underglaze and the white of the porcelain may help to date it."

"The blue looks a little off, like it's greyish, almost messy. I thought it might mean that it's old," Itchy added.

"I need to see it before I can tell you any more. There might be reign marks underneath, for one, which could help to date it. And without a better view of the decoration, and a look at some of the details, like the color of the glaze and the color and condition of the footring and the lid, I can't say if it's old and valuable or not so old and not so valuable."

"I'll see if I can get the seller to let us come over and take a look. I don't know the guy, but he's Chinese and probably local."

"Okay, then call and invite us over. I can join you tomorrow if you want, but I'm off to the States for a week or so the day after."

"Going home?"

"No, this is my home now. I love visiting but Hong Kong suits me better."

"How so?"

"It has the same high energy as New York, same crowded sidewalks and moving people, but things here are more Asian, and that is what I need."

"It's more than the art, isn't it?"

"Yes, it's the culture, the mindset."

"It's a wonder you go back at all."

"Naw, it's still a great city."

"Are you still out on Lantau Island?"

"No. Let me give you my new card," Andy replied, handing one over. It was neatly inscribed with his name—Anderson H. Boyd—and a telephone number, with his Chinese name printed on the reverse side. "I moved into one of those new apartment buildings in Wanchai. I still go out to Lantau several times a week, though."

Andy had moved about six months ago. Wanchai was just west of Central, Hong Kong's downtown district and one of Asia's great money-making machines. People moved to Lantau Island to escape Hong Kong's frenetic pace, but Wanchai's makeover from cheap housing to trendy neighborhood called many back again. According to the local geomancers, the shift came a couple of years after the mirrored glass of I. M. Pei's Bank of China building had reflected some of the good joss, meaning luck or good fortune—and, in this case, meaning money and affluence—from Central to its neighboring district of Wanchai.

"Wanted to be closer to the action?"

"Something like that. Call me when we have a time to view the piece."

* * * *

Andy returned to Ocean Terminal later that afternoon, taking the green and white Star Ferry. He loved the ferry. Where else in the world could you take a ferry for a dime and, in less than two minutes, cross one of the busiest harbors in the world? Once on the Kowloon side, a covered walkway took Andy from the ferry terminal into Ocean Terminal. It was sooner than he expected to return, but Itchy had already called with a time set up for viewing the jar. Andy made it to the shop a few minutes early.

The old-fashioned bell on the front door rang as Andy came in, and Itchy came out from the back of the store.

"Itchy, are you sure that the guy is bringing the jar in this afternoon?" asked Andy. "If it's the real thing, it's going to be really heavy."

"That's what he said," Itchy replied. "I told him my partner—that's you, Andy—wanted to see it too and that it needed to be today or tomorrow."

"It's a bit odd, though, that he is bringing it here—those jars can weigh over a hundred pounds."

Itchy shrugged. They both knew that there was no explaining collectors.

They chatted while they waited. At 4:00 on the dot, two men entered the shop. The first one pulled an old trunk-sized suitcase on wheels. Both men were slim though muscular, and the one pulling the trunk was the bigger of the two. They wore grey cotton pants, black cotton long-sleeved shirts, sneakers with the heels squashed down, and no socks. Local boys, thought Andy, and definitely not the type to own a Yuan dynasty vase.

"You are Mistah Itchy?" demanded the slighter man, looking at Itchy.

"I am," said Itchy.

"And you are Mistah Who?" he inquired, turning to look at Andy.

"Anderson Boyd," Andy replied, handing the man a card from his jacket pocket.

"Where is Mr. Wong?" Itchy asked.

"Mr. Wong no could be here. He send us. He say we show

you suitcase. So, look." The first man had placed the case in front of Andy, then moved back and folded his arms. The second man moved to join him, also crossing his arms.

Andy bent over the case, careful not to present his back to the two men. He opened the lid. The interior was filled with cotton wadding, the industrial kind used for shipping industrial machinery. Inside was indeed a large jar, at least two feet tall. Andy reached for it but was blocked by the bigger man, who plucked it out of the cotton effortlessly, even though it must have weighed over sixty pounds. He moved as though to put it on the dark heavy table to the side. The thinner man picked up the vase that was already on the table—Mrs. Carmichael's special—and started to move it to another table. He looked at Itchy and gestured with it to the new location.

"Okay?" he asked.

"Sure, make yourself at home," invited Itchy with a laugh.

The bigger man set the jar on the table, and both men resumed their places near the door, arms folded.

"So, what are your names?" asked Itchy to the men. They shrugged.

"Okay," said Itchy, "Let's try an easier topic. Will Mr. Wong be joining us?"

The slighter man shook his head.

"But you guys work for Mr. Wong?" Itchy asked, getting a little nervous. The two Chinese guys looked at each other and smiled slightly. They said nothing.

"Where does he work? Mr. Wong? I mean what does he do?" Itchy tried again. The two looked at each other then looked at Andy, who was busy looking inside and under the jar. He was feeling the weight of it and closely examining the glaze.

This time, Itchy threw his hands in the air and conceded defeat.

"There is a lid? A top?" Andy motioned like he was putting a top on the jar.

The heavier set guy understood and nodded, reaching back into the box and removing the lid. He placed it on the table next to the jar.

"What do you guys do for Mr. Wong?" Itchy tried again, never daunted for long.

The two guys looked at each other again and then looked at Andy. The thin one said, "He asks a lot of questions."

Andy glanced at Itchy and then at the other two men and said, "Yes, he's from Brooklyn, where everyone is convinced they are likeable. Mr. Carmichael can't help himself."

The two Chinese guys looked at each other. One nodded while the other shrugged.

Andy circled the table, taking in all sides of the jar. The color, as Itchy had described, was mostly greyish, but on closer examination revealed brownish-red patches with very rare bits of dark red, all on a white background. It was not blue at all. Andy had his game face on, calm and unrevealing. He reached over for his digital camera. "Okay if I take some pictures?"

"Mr. Wong say okay for pictures," said the thinner one, the voluble one.

Andy shot a dozen pictures, turning the piece. Then he said, "Okay, I'm done."

Andy motioned to the two guys that they could put the jar back in the trunk. They picked it up.

"Wait," interrupted Andy, motioning with his hands for the two to hold the jar on its side before it was placed in the trunk. The two paused, and Andy leaned over to examine the bottom. He took a quick snapshot.

Andy then ran his finger along the bottom surface. He nodded, and the jar went into the trunk.

In perfect Cantonese, Andy said to them, "Please thank Mr. Wong and tell him we will be in touch very soon."

The two guys looked at each other in surprise, and Andy followed up with a colloquial Cantonese expression: "One does not discard an oyster without first looking for a pearl."

Without blinking, the heavier guy said in Cantonese, "You sound like my old grandfather." The two men laughed as they left the shop. Once out the door, they spoke to each other in rapid Chinese.

"What did you say to them?" Itchy burst out.

"I said that we would be in touch with Mr. Wong very soon," replied Andy.

"And that made them laugh like that?" Itchy Yitsy asked incredulously.

"No," Andy said. "I used a local expression: 'One does not discard an oyster without first looking for a pearl.'"

Itchy looked puzzled.

"It translates to something like, 'Don't judge a book by its cover,'" Andy explained. "I was chiding him for assuming I knew nothing about anything Chinese just because I looked like a white man."

"And how did he take it?" Itchy asked.

"He said I sounded just like his old grandfather," Andy said, considering for a moment. "A very nice compliment I might add."

Itchy smiled in understanding.

"They certainly warmed up at the end," he commented.

"Mmm," was Andy's reply.

"So, now you have seen it. What do you think?" Itchy demanded, oblivious to Andy's inattentiveness.

"It's a world class object," Andy replied, almost against his will. "It's beautiful, splendid. The jar is in excellent condition, no cracks or breaks. Well, there are minor cracks in the body at the bottom, on the foot, but that is right, because this is a big, heavy pot, and the weight of it would have split the clay as it sat and began to be fired. This is a very important jar, possibly the only one like it in the world."

"So it's the real thing?" asked Itchy.

"Well, the potting is right, and the thickness of clay and overall weight are what they should be. I checked the bottom, and there were no marks—another good thing. The Jingdezhen kilns did not put marks on the bottom during the early Ming, so the absence of marks is a good sign. Reign marks weren't initiated until later in the Ming dynasty during the fifteenth century, with the fourth Ming emperor Xuande. I also felt the bottom around the footring, which was free of glaze."

"Why is that good? Why not apply glaze all over?" asked Itchy.

"If you added glaze to the bottom and fired it, it would bake to the bottom of the kiln—a bad thing, don't you think?" Andy replied, and Itchy smiled. Andy continued.

"I think it was made in the fourteenth century. And even the lid looks original, not a later replacement. That's what really makes it one of a kind."

"What about the mottled color? The murky blue?" asked Itchy.

"That's what's so incredible—it isn't blue at all, it's red."

"Red?" asked Itchy. "I've never heard of such a thing. Is it recent?"

"Copper red, actually, and no, the real stuff isn't recent at all. If it's real, the color is perfect—the glaze color is actually quite good for the period," said Andy, still amazed by what he had seen. "The uneven color is another piece in the puzzle—the imperial kilns at Jingdezhen could not control the copper-red glaze until well into the fourteenth century, and even then it remained too volatile to produce in large quantities. These kilns used superior fine white porcelaneous clay, achieving a whiter color in the background, with the red glaze fading to grey on the body after firing. If the color had been uniformly grey or uniformly red, it would probably be a more recent piece."

"There are a few of these pots on this scale in museums," continued Andy. "Two in Asia, two in Europe, and one in the US. I've seen them, even the one in Shanghai. But none of them have an original lid. This is not something that just appears." Andy shook his head.

"Are you thinking it might be stolen?"

"I have no idea. It could be stolen, or it could be looted from some location in China. Of course, it could also be a legitimate family heirloom."

"What do you think it's worth?" asked Itchy.

"Who knows? You can't easily price this kind of object, but someone could easily be willing to pay seven figures for it. Whatever someone will pay," he added, "you don't really see this kind of thing on the market very often. If it is legit, this is really world class museum quality, actually beyond the reach of most museums."

Andy looked at Itchy and became very serious. "Perhaps, we should speak again with our mysterious Mr. Wong. Where on earth did he get this?"

"I can call him, I have the number. I don't know where he lives though. The telephone number is an exchange used for mobile phones," Itchy offered.

"Shall I give it a try?" asked Andy.

"Let me call him first. He seems skittish to me. He okayed my bringing in a partner to look at the jar, but he is being very mysterious." Itchy was starting to sound nervous himself.

Andy added soberly, "And I don't know what to think of the two goons—they look like local muscle, but they were here on such a pedestrian task. They look too big for house servants."

CHAPTER
2

ndy began the next day as he always did, with sit-ups, push-ups, and stretches, beginning with his head and working down to his feet. It was his wake-up and warm-up before a short run and martial arts workout.

When Andy lived out on Lantau Island, he had a lot of open space to practice his martial arts. More important, his Sifu, Chen Xiaohu—pronounced she-ow-who—lived on Lantau. Sifu's name translated into Little Tiger Chen, the last name Mandarin in spelling and sound. The Cantonese form of the name would be Chan, another common family name, but Xiaohu insisted on the Mandarin version. Andy had practiced with his teacher almost every day when he lived on Lantau, but now, with a commute on the hydrofoil from Central out to Lantau, he practiced three days a week.

They had been together for more than a dozen years, ever since Andy moved to Hong Kong with little other than his degrees in East Asian art history and literature. Two years ago, Andy himself became a master in martial arts. Over time, he had become one of his teacher's closest students.

Andy's formal study of the martial arts started in his teens, when his parents signed him up for karate as a way to harness, or deplete, his constant energy. His informal study had commenced years earlier as a boy watching Keith Carradine on TV. Andy loved the endless march up and down the training hall doing kicks and punches, but he found similar delight in the reading assignments given by his Japanese teacher, or Sensei. He soaked up the discipline both physical and mental, and the more he absorbed the lessons, the more he thrived. He employed his focus in the other areas of his life, such as his study habits. He adopted respectful manners more typical of Asian children. Likely his parents would have paid more than they did for the karate lessons had they understood the added benefits.

Mostly, he assimilated the Asian perspective that he was part of a larger community, one worth serving, which set him apart from the "me" perspective more common in American youth. By the time he reached college, Andy had a sense of belonging, of his place in the world, that most people didn't find until their later thirties.

In college, Andy concentrated on the culture of East Asia—its religions, philosophies, literature, and art. He found many Asian friends at Harvard, and it felt natural to move back with some of them when they returned to Hong Kong. Soon after, he heard of an extraordinary martial arts teacher in Lantau, and he was on his way. They had been together ever since.

* * * *

Andy just made the 5:32 a.m. ferry to Lantau from the Central terminal on the harbor's edge. It was the first out on a weekday. The cab drivers at Mui Wo, or Silvermine Bay, on the Lantau side knew Andy, as he was pretty much the only passenger who needed a ride at that hour. His ride took him along the southern road, near the Shek Pik Reservoir. Sifu lived farther west, on the Ngong Ping Plateau, in the small town around the Po Lin Monastery. The Po Lin Monastery was home to the Giant Buddha, a huge bronze considered the largest outdoor seated Buddha in China and a popular tourist attraction. The Monastery did not open to the public until 10:00 a.m., however, so the hordes had yet to arrive.

Lantau was roughly twice the size of Hong Kong Island, and about half of its land was devoted to national parks. It was sparsely populated by Asian standards, however, with plenty of empty green mountains and scrublands. Incidentally, it boasted the cheapest housing in the area.

Over the years, workout sessions with his teacher were always in the same place. They had given a name to the plateau in Southern Lantau Park where they met: "Viewing the Tao Plateau." The Chinese loved to give every little piece of land a poetic name. In a traditional Chinese garden, virtually every doorway, pagoda, and hallway had a poetic name. It was just the Chinese way. Andy used to joke with his family about naming the garage door or the door to the tool shed or the shed itself. They never got it.

In any case, the cabbies all knew where Andy was going at that hour. He was dropped at the edge of the park and he walked and jogged in. Andy loved working out in the same place time after time, seeing the sun rise each time. It was never the same twice. Sometimes it was misty, sometimes cloudy, sometimes clear, but the combination of sun, sea, wind, and clouds differed every day.

A handful of Sifu's best, most advanced students waited together for the lesson: Danny Chung, Tommy Lee, and Peter Tsui. Danny and Tommy both lived on Lantau Island. Tommy lived to the north in Discovery Bay, home to many foreign nationals and their families. Danny lived in the apartment complexes farther west in Tung Ching. Peter came over from Hong Kong Island, often riding the ferry with Andy. Last night he must have come out in the early evening, eating and staying at Tommy's.

They all had Chinese names, as did Andy, but went by half Western, half Chinese names. Danny and Tommy were both from

Hong Kong, while Peter was born in Taiwan and had moved to Hong Kong with his family when he was a kid. The four students, including Andy, were of comparable rank, and the years had bound them together like brothers, in some ways closer than blood relatives.

"I'm not the last to arrive?" asked Andy in surprise.

"Not this morning," said Danny.

"Maybe waiting is part of the lesson," offered Andy. The others smiled at him. He was the only non-Chinese student and the youngest by a few months, though he was treated like everyone's kid brother.

"It's another lesson to make you more Chinese," said Peter.

Despite the energy and activity of Hong Kong, many Chinese still had a different sense of time and a disdain for rushing anything. Westerners, particularly Americans, offended without realizing it, with their can-do attitudes. Andy supposed it came from having several thousand years of culture and history, which fostered a different, leisurely sense of time.

"My family in the United States think I've become too Chinese," noted Andy.

"You know what you are?" demanded Peter. "You are a hard-boiled egg!"

Andy resigned himself to the punch line.

"You are white on the outside and yellow in the inside!"

The four laughed, even Andy, at the analogy. It wasn't inaccurate; Andy had a Westerner's facade but an Asian's mindset, certainly more than his face and speech would indicate.

Chen Xiaohu appeared a few feet away, approaching silently.

Sifu's students never knew what the lesson would be about. Some days it was purely about physical movement, about the subtleties of turning one's hand in a particular way to manifest different kinds of *qi*. *Qi*, that energy that permeates the universe, can be directed and controlled by anyone with a little guidance and a lot of practice. And Sifu gave them a lot of practice. Or, the lesson might be about balance in life—that physical, spiritual, and intellectual training and practice should be in proper proportions, and that an extreme of any one of the three would put the other two in danger of imbalance.

In one lesson, Sifu described how the forms practiced reflected their characters, revealing who they were at that very moment. When Sifu told one of the students to change the way in which he did a particular form, to modify it, he was, in fact, telling him to modify his life in the same way.

Their Sifu was a small man of tremendous energy and enthusiasms. He had average features but such huge vitality that he was easily noticed in a crowd, unless he didn't want to be. He was the kind of man for whom space was made, be it in the form of a seat on the train, a chair in a restaurant, or a bench in a park.

Today's lesson covered a meditative and qigong energy exercise based on the "brush knee" posture in taiji quan. In this posture, students created a ring with their arms and hands in front of their chest, palms inward, like they were holding a tree trunk, a posture sometimes referred to as the "jade belt" posture. Within this ring, the students imagined a pool of energy. By moving their arms in and out, they expanded and contracted the ring as well as the rings of energy. Then, they dipped one hand each into this energy lake, scooped up some energy, and let it wash over their hearts and faces, past the ear where they "listened." Next, they struck out with the open hand, while all the energy drained out of the other hand, which had fallen just off the hip. The opposite hand then curved back and turned over to dip into the pool of energy again, and the sequence repeated, alternating the hands. Eventually, the movements became quick and fluid. The group then practiced several "forms," specific series of movements in their entirety, together just conscious of the rising sun.

These postures required practice to understand all the subtleties fully, and the so-called brothers asked questions and chatted afterwards. The camaraderie was easy and today they conversed lightly, arranging to go to breakfast together, save for Andy.

"Andy," inquired Danny Chung, "are you ill? You are not clamoring for your next meal?"

Andy grinned at the teasing. "I'll eat on the ferry." His friend laughed. "I have to return to Hong Kong. I'm leaving for New York tomorrow."

"Who did you find to pay for this junket?" asked Peter. As a freelance consultant on Chinese art, Andy went where the work called.

"I have two jobs lined up: I am writing an exhibition catalog for an auction house, and yes, Peter, the auction house is paying my way. I have another job, too, a smaller one to appraise an estate collection of Asian art."

"How do you find these people?" asked Peter.

"They find me. I've worked in the past for the auction house owner. He liked my work and offered me this bigger job." His friends hooted good-naturedly at this. "Because I will be in New York City, I agreed to take the other job, which came to me from one of my college buddies who is now a well-respected lawyer and working on settling an estate."

His friend, Doug Winston, represented the deceased collector. He required hard numbers from an independent appraiser because the heirs were at war over individual pieces. Andy looked forward to seeing Doug again, while satisfying his exaggerated curiosity about people's collections.

Sifu knew already that Andy would be traveling to the US, and he gave Andy a few small wrapped gifts and some photographs to deliver to a relative in Flushing, Queens. The others threatened to load him down with gifts for their own stateside relatives. Everyone in Hong Kong had a relative in Queens. Andy bore the teasing with good will, bowing to Sifu and saying the traditional "Thank you for teaching us."

"Ah, Andy," started Sifu.

"Yes, is there something else?"

"I need you to help me with something when you get back, a small art project."

"It would be my honor," noted Andy seriously.

"I have a painting from my brother that needs some attention—just the job for you," said Sifu.

Andy bowed again, pleased to be able to assist Sifu.

* * * *

Andy had an eye for beauty and he saw it everywhere, a trait that only helped him in the art world. It didn't fail him that morning either, when he returned to his building. Just to the right of the entrance, a long, marbled concierge desk, equipped with telephone and intercom controls and shelves in the back to store packages and deliveries, took up most of the lobby entryway. On the left of the lobby was a small seating area for guests to wait, a small carpet, two comfortable chairs, and a glass table with a silk flower arrangement. Beyond were the mailroom and the bank of elevators. None of these features caught Andy's eye, but he always greeted the staff on duty and made a point to know each person's name.

As Andy turned to the right to greet Wong Hei, the morning concierge, a woman came out of the elevators and passed Andy on his left. He glanced at her and noticed that she was as tall as he was, but it was her profile that sent him back. Fantastic, he thought, and right off an old Roman coin. An aquiline nose in the middle of Hong Kong—now that was a real find. She didn't appear to notice him, and in another moment she was out the door and lost in the crowded sidewalk.

"Fabulous," he said to Wong Hei. "Does she live here?"

"Good morning, Mistah Boyd. Have a good day," replied Wong Hei, who never discussed the other tenants.

* * * *

The phone rang around two in the afternoon. Itchy said, "Hey, Andy. It's Itchy."

"What did he say?" Andy asked.

"He didn't say much at all, and talked even less about where it came from. He just wanted to know if we were interested, and he'd like the answer fast."

"Well, we certainly are interested."

"Then he wants a million dollars for it, in a nice quiet sale."

"Wow, he must think it's an interesting piece, too."

"Too much?" asked Itchy.

"Not necessarily, assuming you really owned it after you handed over the money."

"You still think it might be stolen?" Itchy repeated his earlier question.

The both knew that stolen art changed hands all the time. Too many collectors were willing to buy stolen art outright, no questions asked, and put it in their private collections. Many dealers participated—the money was too good to ignore—but Itchy and Andy did not fall into that group. They both had come too far and worked too hard to risk their reputations.

"I think we need to look into it. I'll ask around and do some research. I'd be happier if we found a reference to it in some art collection. I'll start with some friends and contacts in New York."

he next morning, Andy worked out in Hong Kong. He had favorite workout spots near his new home: on the waterfront along the harbor and in Victoria Park. In the middle of summer, he worked out in the relative cool of early morning before it got too hot, preferring the water-front for its harbor breezes. Even with humidity at 110 percent, Andy thought it beat snow every time. During the rainy season, April through September, there was a big open-air roofed pagoda that provided protection in Victoria Park. Neither location was as scenic as Lantau.

At 5:00 a.m., it was still a beautiful, clear October morning. If he stayed in Central, Andy would jog to Victoria Park and begin his martial arts with qigong breathing exercises. These deep-breathing exercises coordinated breathing with movements of the hands and helped to focus the mind and body. They also stimulated the *qi*, or intrinsic energy. He practiced and taught all styles of taiji quan, and other practitioners often approached to ask questions or to discuss different techniques, but not today.

Andy took the early afternoon flight, which got him to the US a few hours later in the afternoon on the same day. It took sixteen hours to complete the trip, and this was the shorter route that went over the top of the earth to Chicago, rather than around the fat part of the globe through San Francisco. He would stop in Chicago, collect his bags and clear customs, and re-check his bags for the last leg to New York.

Andy had plenty of time to think about the Chinese jar. He took out the digital photographs that he'd printed out before he left. That it had a lid was a strong selling point, as most lids were broken over time.

The color was remarkable—those blues that "didn't work." Itchy was way off when he thought the imperfections in the "blues" meant that the jar would not be valuable. Cobalt blue pigment could manifest a range of colors after firing, but cobalt was a fairly stable pigment, which explained its widespread use. This blue was best known for the blue and white porcelains of the Ming dynasty, much of it imported from Persia until indigenous sources were discovered.

Andy had read up a bit on red glazes before he left. He recalled that copper-red glaze was used for a very short time in the fourteenth century, either in the late Yuan dynasty, which ended in 1368, or in the early Ming dynasty, which began when the Yuan ended. Andy thought it most likely that it was used when the first emperor of the Ming dynasty shut down all trade with Persia and the rest of the world, so that imported cobalt was no longer available and copper red was tried as a replacement color.

In any case, it was used only for about twenty years or so at the famous imperial kilns located at Jingdezhen. Even less was known about the formula for the glaze or where the copper oxide, the key ingredient, came from. This glaze was notoriously difficult to control, often turning more grey than red, with a tendency to pool and crack in places. There were no pieces of any kind that were all red, and the best of them showed grey traces or reddish-grey colors.

Andy looked at the picture again. The pot was about twenty-four inches tall. The bands of decoration around the pot appeared typical of the late Yuan period. The great Mongolian empire, which was begun by Genghis Khan and lasted throughout the thirteenth and fourteenth centuries, stretched from Korea to Hungary. Two of Genghis Khan's grandsons formed a close alliance and ran large sections of the empire. By the mid-thirteenth century, Kublai Khan in China had begun the Yuan dynasty, while his cousin Hulegu began the Ilkhanid dynasty in Persia. Under Yuan dynasty manufacture, cobalt blue oxide was imported from Persia and joined with the fine white clay of China into ceramic vessels of all shapes, and then exported back to Persia. The Persian style included dense and scrolling floral and plant motifs, and Persian designs typically left no undecorated space on any jar or plate. It was not until the Ming that the more typical and less crowded Chinese style of decoration came to dominate. It was rather ironic that the so-called Ming dynasty blue and white ceramics were originally made during the Yuan dynasty for a non-Chinese—specifically, Persian—audience.

This jar had nine registers, or bands, of decoration and no empty space, signaling Yuan period influence. If it were indeed a copper glaze jar from the Yuan period, and one so large at that, it would be one of only three or four in the world. Each of the other known examples resided in museum collections in Tokyo, New York, London, and Shanghai. None of those had an original lid, which meant that if this was genuine, it was the only one like it in the world. Now that would be a find.

"How is it possible that something like this was not known?" Andy murmured to himself. "Why did the owner choose Itchy of all people to sell something he obviously knew nothing about?"

Andy put the photograph back in his bag and snoozed for about six hours, waking in time for the last wake-up meal before arriving in Chicago. It was a fairly short time until he was taking off again on the last leg of the trip to New York City.

The first thing he noticed at LaGuardia was that he wasn't the tallest person anymore. Then he noticed he was tired, hungry, and maybe a little cranky. "Am I more jet lagged going this way or going the other way?" he asked himself. "Now that's a federal government study worth funding."

Andy stood on line for a cab, which took its place in the slow snake of traffic moving north and west on the Grand Central Parkway, the main artery from the airport into Manhattan. It still didn't feel like home, yet, or even a homecoming.

* * * *

Andy left his bags at his hotel on Forty-second Street and found the subway to the Upper East Side. He got out at Eighty-sixth Street and walked three long blocks west to Fifth Avenue, turning down again on Museum Mile, the stretch of city street that housed a dozen museums. In three blocks, he came to the Manhattan Museum of Art.

It was a sunny, clear day, one of those warm October days that fooled you into wearing a light coat even though you'd be cold after sundown. This stretch of Fifth Avenue had Central Park on one side beyond the high stonewall, and gracious pre-war apartment buildings on the other. The leaves in the park had started to turn, so yellows, oranges, and red mixed in with the green. Andy was suddenly reminded of autumnal collages, one of those projects that every child in the northeastern United States had to complete before third grade. And oak tag—Andy savored the words, the odd name for the poster board on which the leaves were glued then labeled.

Sometimes Andy missed the changes in the seasons, the different temperatures, the way the air changed from the loamy smell of spring, or the crisp, dry smell of right before it snowed.

Andy shook his head and rejoined the present. Coming upon the Museum on his right, Andy felt this was, possibly, one of the most civilized places in Manhattan. The huge stairs leading to the main entrance were jammed with people, natives and tourists who knew better than to squander such a lovely day. He scanned the faces, looking for Adrienne Strosser, an assistant curator in the Asian Department. Adrienne was warm and funny, an expert in East Asian lacquer, conversant in four or five languages, and, best of all, blessed with the power to recommend acquisitions directly to the director. Most assistant curators had no access to the director, but Adrienne's family had donated a fair number of Old Master paintings and drawings over the years. Her family had recognized her keen mind and "good eye" for great art and encouraged her career as an art historian.

Adrienne was sitting at the top of the stairs on one of the sets of stone benches beneath the huge columns, with her face tilted to the sun. It was a good face, oval with regular features framed by curly, shoulder-length hair. She wore classic outfits, typical of old, quiet-money families, grey slacks and a cream twin set. She broke ranks with her jewelry, wearing a minor Moghul necklace and bracelet, Victorian-era jewelry from India made of square gold links that were enameled and set with semi-precious, rough-cut stones. Jewelry wasn't Andy's specialty, but he knew enough about East Asian artisans to recognize top quality pieces like Adrienne's. Eager to impress her with his linguistic skills, he greeted her in German.

"Gezundheit," she replied, opening her eyes and smiling in welcome.

"That bad?" asked Andy in dismay. Andy put a hand on her shoulder and bent to kiss her cheek. He was in America again, where it was customary to show affection to friends.

"Well, happily, you live in Hong Kong, and not Dusseldorf. What brings you around during my break?" Andy had called her that morning, asking her to give him a few minutes, quietly.

"I just wanted to sit on the stairs here and show the world I am an intellectual," replied Andy, as he dropped down on the bench next to her.

"Yes, the stairs magically transform even you into an instant intellectual," grinned Adrienne.

"Why, yes, I come here all the time," added Andy in a high falsetto. "It's really the only decent place to read Proust," he joked.

"Actually, I'm in town for a couple of projects, among them an estate appraisal. The estate has some really good pieces, I hear— a few of them museum quality, including a few Chinese and Japanese paintings and a small South East Asian bronze Maitreya. I thought I'd give you the heads-up."

"Hmmm," she replied.

"I haven't seen it yet, but I was told there is a nice Chinese painting that the Museum might want, a landscape by Wen Zhengming."

Adrienne hummed again. "Provenance? Any problems with it?" she asked.

"It has been in the family's private collection since the 1920s. There are loads of paper on each purchase and likely a copy of the original bill of sale."

"Has it been recorded as being outside of China before 1970?" she inquired, referring to the year of the UNESCO agreement. UNESCO marked the first real effort to hold museums to a standard of care to ensure that they were not buying looted objects. And lately there had been a lot of press about repatriating stolen art to Europe.

"I don't think there will be a looting issue," replied Andy, going to the heart of the matter. "It looks like a legitimate purchase from the 1920s."

"Yeah," she laughed, "that was a nice stable period in China, notable for regularized commercial transactions."

"Now, now," chided Andy. "It's how a lot of museums in this country acquired great Chinese objects. And yes, many enterprises prospered during the Warlord period."

"Sure, that's why twenty-six different local paper currencies were printed."

The warlords were always in dire need of money, and some resorted to printing their own paper. Within a specific local area the paper had value, but very few were recognized farther afield.

Andy smiled in acknowledgment. "As I said, there is a bill of sale, and I will look at the seals and inscription."

"Let's just be sure," cautioned Adrienne. "We don't want any more Cambodian heads or Rembrandt drawings."

Andy understood the reference. Last year, the Museum had returned a tenth century head of Shiva that had been looted from Cambodia and smuggled out of the country. And two months later, a Rembrandt drawing of a lion that had been "acquired" by the Nazis was tracked down by the heirs of the original owner to the Museum's collection. Although the Museum had received both as gifts and believed they were legitimately purchased years before, the objects were returned to the Cambodian government and the Austrian heirs. The press had created such a stink that all the curators were ordered to be overly cautious.

"Does the Museum still have the large red and white bowl on display?" Andy asked, changing the subject slightly.

Adrienne looked at him a moment and nodded.

"Since when do you do pots?" she asked.

"I do whatever my clients want me to do," noted Andy. "I need some advice on red and white pieces."

"Well, aren't you in luck, then. A couple of museum technicians are rotating some of the ceramics in that case this morning. If we're lucky, the case is still open and we can take a look. Let's take a walk through the gallery upstairs, and I'll give you some pointers."

They walked through the main doors, past the round information desk, and toward the back of the rotunda. The two-story rotunda was the hub off of which branched the other galleries and wings. On the first floor, the Egyptian wing was to the right, Greco Roman to the left. In back, the graceful marble steps led up to the second floor. Chinese ceramics lined the walls around this mezzanine. Thousands of visitors passed them, usually on the way to a special exhibit, failing to give the ceramics their due. On the second floor, over the Egyptian wing, lay the rest of the Asian galleries.

As Andy and Adrienne approached the main staircase, Adrienne reached over the side of the ticket booth to snare brightly-colored metal circle-badges. Andy bent his to secure it to his shirt collar.

"Now I'm officially a guest," he noted.

They mounted the stairs together.

"It never gets old, walking up these stairs," noted Adrienne.

"It's an elegant staircase," agreed Andy.

"It's the old world charm—it works for me every time," said Adrienne. Andy smiled his agreement.

Upstairs, large folding screens hid the case on the back wall. Two technicians talked softly behind the screens.

"Knock, knock," said Adrienne as she pushed open one side of a screen, revealing two technicians surrounded by three carts. One was empty and the other held more porcelains.

"Good morning," she said. They recognized her and smiled. "Morning," they both replied. Andy was introduced and the technicians returned to what they were doing. The large red and white bowl with its uneven glaze sat in the case with other marvelous porcelains.

Adrienne plucked the bowl out of the case and set it down on an empty padded cart. "It should say on the label text, 'Hey! I'm not a potter's mistake! It's really hard to control this red glaze!'" noted Adrienne. "See how the red never really obtains a solid red color, it's always a greyish muddy tone, and then it fades to all grey, almost in patches. The lines are never crisp. It was really no more than a potting experiment to replace cobalt blue in the early Ming."

"It's not late Yuan period?" Andy asked.

"No. Scholars in the past dated it possibly late Yuan, but now everyone in the field places it later in time, at early Ming."

"Why?" asked Andy.

"The first emperor of the Ming, Hongwu, shut down all trade for two decades, including trade to and from Persia, which is where cobalt oxide came from. Artisans tried to replace the blue with copper oxide," Adrienne responded.

Andy nodded. "And no reign mark, right?"

"Yes," she confirmed. She picked up the bowl and turned it over, placing the bowl face down. "This one doesn't have reign marks. It was made during the Hongwu period, which ended in 1401. Reign marks began to appear during his grandson Xuande's reign some forty years later. Also, it's pretty heavy. Go ahead and pick it up. But please, be very careful."

Andy nodded again and carefully picked up the bowl to get a sense of its weight. He was sensible of the absolute trust Adrienne placed in him. Non-staff at the Museum simply did not pick up irreplaceable fifteenth-century bowls. Andy was careful, lifting the bowl and holding it for a moment to feel its full weight. He placed it back down and put his face very close to the bowl to get a good look at the glaze up close. Then he ran his fingers over the glaze, committing the feel of it to memory. Andy had the ability to store these observations on his own internal hard drive and to find the right data again on demand. It was one reason he was good at what he did. "This is fantastic. Thank you so much for letting me see this," said Andy.

"There aren't very many of these," she added, almost joking. "There simply aren't that many good pieces, not on this scale."

"Are there any large jars that have a lid intact?" Andy asked.

"No, none with the original lids, at least not in any museum or collection I've heard about. Why, do you have one?" she asked, looking right at him. "It sounds like you've seen a red and white piece lately. Just a second." She turned to the two technicians, who were now watching the two of them, and said, "Thanks guys. Can you put it back?" They both nodded as Adrienne led Andy out the way they came.

"I don't know what I have. I'm not sure if my client is that lucky, and I'm really not sure where it might have come from," Andy replied. He reached into his bag and pulled out an envelope, which he handed to Adrienne.

She pulled out the photographs. "Holy cow," she said.

"Yes," Andy agreed.

"Genuine?" she asked. It was an obvious question that revealed her instinct that the piece was genuine.

"I just don't know," replied Andy truthfully.

"Try the auction houses," suggested Adrienne, as she handed back the photographs. "Someone with a good memory may remember this kind of jar."

"Okay, thanks. I'll be in touch. I definitely owe you," Andy said as he turned to walk down the staircase.

* * * *

Back on the Fifth Avenue sidewalk, Andy took out his mobile phone and dialed his friend Toni Case. It was now after 6:00, but he took a chance that this workaholic would still be in the office. Toni was a specialist in Chinese ceramics at a large auction house nearby, and Andy had befriended her when she lived in Hong Kong for a couple of years as part of her training. Independent experts like Andy needed to cultivate, and keep, friends everywhere.

"Hi Toni, Andy Boyd," Andy said.

"Hey, Andy. Where are you?" Toni responded cheerily.

"Long time no see. I'm in New York for a short time and thought I'd give you a call. I actually have a professional question, too."

"Okay, shoot," she replied. Toni was a very focused, very serious member of the Asian Art Department. She treated all inquiries with equal gravity and never made anyone feel the interruption was unwelcome.

"Have you ever heard anything about a large copper-red jar, one with an original lid?" Andy asked.

Toni sucked in her breath. "No." She thought for a moment, reviewing her own encyclopedic memory. "I have never even heard of one with an original lid. If it were really good, it would be worth a small fortune. This past spring at auction we sold a large blue and white jar, about eighteen inches tall, that had a lid. Let's see, it was early Ming, Hongwu period, maybe the last decade of the fourteenth century, and a lovely example. We got 1.5 million dollars US for it. What aren't you telling me? Where did you find it? Is anyone selling it?"

"I haven't found it yet, but as my mother would say, hope springs eternal," Andy quipped.

"Okay, mister inscrutable kung fu master. You let me know and give us a chance to make it worth your while."

"I know, I know, the usual finder's fee. I'll let you know if it turns into anything. Let's try to have a drink while I'm here."

"I'm kind of swamped right now getting our next catalogue ready. Can you call me in a day or two?" Toni asked.

"Will do," Andy said, and he flipped the phone shut.

The following morning, Andy took the 7 train from mid-town Manhattan to Flushing, Queens, to pay his respects to his Sifu's cousin and to give him the gifts and photos. Andy felt slightly out of sorts. The time change kept him awake late into the night, and he knew he would become sleepy again later in the morning. Worst yet, he could not decide what meal he was hungry for.

After appropriate greetings, Chen Wenbeng informed Andy that Chen Xiaohu had been taken to the hospital the day before after vomiting and collapsing with severe pains in his abdomen.

Andy was stunned.

"It seems he could not reach you directly," offered Chen Wenbeng. "One of your friends, Danny Chung, called here because he knew you would be here soon."

Andy pulled out his mobile phone. While it worked in both Hong Kong and the US, it would only work if the battery was charged. "My phone battery went dead," said Andy softly. "I didn't notice. I'm sorry you were left to take my messages."

"I also wanted to know that my cousin was so ill," Chen Wenbeng reminded him. Andy stayed for another hour, bringing Chen Wenbeng up to date on changes in Hong Kong. He gave Chen

Wenbeng his hotel telephone number and asked him to call or leave a message if anything changed with Sifu.

* * * *

Andy returned from Flushing on the subway, transferring at Grand Central Terminal for the express train again to the Upper East Side. This time he got out at Fifty-ninth Street and walked only as far as Park Avenue.

Andy met Doug Winston in the lobby of a quietly affluent building on Park Avenue. Mid-height and stocky, Doug hadn't changed much. He was maybe a bit more respectable, but still had the friendly, warm face that Andy remembered. Under the disapproving gaze of the concierge, their greetings were suitably muted and they rode up the wood-paneled elevator in silence. The elevator opened on a small vestibule serving two apartments, and Doug had the key to the collector's apartment. It was a spacious prewar with three bedrooms and two maids' rooms. "Plenty of room for a collector," Andy noted to himself.

"It's been too long," said Doug.

"More than ten years," agreed Andy.

"I was delighted when your name came up in reference to this job. I hadn't realized that you stayed in Asian art. I remember you were crazy for the stuff at Harvard. And you live in Hong Kong. What's that like?" Doug asked, as they entered the apartment.

Andy thought for a second. "It has worked out nicely for me. In the last decade there have been major shifts in the international art scene, beginning with New York, which took first place away from London in several major sectors of the art market, like contemporary and Old Masters. One of the biggest and oldest auction houses established in London three hundred years ago in fact moved their world headquarters to New York. Auction houses follow the money, and during the 1990s it was in New York."

"The entire Asian art market has shifted to New York—that is, all except Chinese art," Andy continued. "There are major markets in Asia—Beijing for contemporary art and Hong Kong for everything Chinese. But really, since the handover to China, Hong Kong has become the center for Chinese painting, which is my first love. In this area, the large auction houses in New York pretty much moved their divisions to Hong Kong. They still have previews of objects in New York, but the actual sales occur in Hong Kong. This has been great for me—I've been there since before the art market boomed and I've established myself in the community. I do a steady business now with a number of Western collectors, who rely on me to find paintings or other Asian art for them. Sometimes I attend the auctions and bid for customers who are too busy to make the trip all the way to Hong Kong."

"Can't someone just buy it from a catalog?" asked Doug.

"It's important to see the object in person, or to appoint a proxy, someone who may verify authenticity, react to the art in person, touch it, and examine it. And I get to spend my days pursuing lovely things."

"Speaking of which," Doug said, making a sweeping motion with his hand and walking into the living room.

"Yes, now, do you want a piece-by-piece valuation or just the bottom line?" Andy asked with a more serious look on his face.

"Oh, we need a piece-by-piece valuation, with as much supporting data as possible because the three heirs, the collector's three children, are squabbling like mad over everything. It's a final revenge against a man who preferred his art to his children, with the winner getting the most valuable piece and therefore the largest allotment of love." Doug shook his head at the folly.

"That bad?"

"They almost came to blows over this Chinese screen," said Doug, pointing to the multi-paneled screen on the inside wall.

"Japanese."

"Eh?"

"It's a Japanese screen."

"You can tell that just with a glance?"

"Yes," Andy smiled. "Yes, because although the Chinese invented the screen as a format, for whatever reason they lost their enthusiasm for it. The Japanese, on the other hand, embraced the idea and perfected the folding screen format you're admiring there."

Andy walked over to it. It was a six-panel screen of birds and flowers. There was an inscription, a signature, and a large red seal in the bottom left corner.

"It's probably half of a pair of screens with birds and flowers of the four seasons," Andy said, as he switched on his art history voice. "Look at the snow on the bamboo on the two far-left panels, and then look at the red maple leaves and chrysanthemums on the right panels. Reading from right to left, you are looking at the autumn and winter sections. There was probably another six-panel screen made at the same time that depicted the birds and flowers of the Spring and Summer screen. It's painted with ink and color on paper. There is an inscription in Japanese that reads 'painted by Shoei' and a signature that reads 'Tanyu' and a seal."

"What you have here, if it's genuine, is a sixteenth-century screen painted during the late Muromachi period in Japan—that's the late fourteenth century through the end of the sixteenth century. The artist Shoei was one of the lesser-known painters of the very famous Kano school of painters, and Tanyu, one of the most famous of the later Kano school painters, lived a hundred years later and was something like the great-grandson of Shoei."

Doug was impressed and said, "You really know your stuff. You are definitely the right guy for the job."

"The signature and the seal alone aren't confirmation. They may have been added later by someone else attempting to fabricate a good provenance for the painting. However, the painting technique seems right, by which I mean that the manner in which the brushstrokes are applied seems right, and the ink and paper look right. I'll look up other examples of the calligraphy in the inscription and signature as well as the seal to confirm authenticity. It may even be possible to locate the other screen. You never know. For me that's part of the fun—knowing where to hunt for information and putting together the pieces."

"Will it be valuable?" asked Doug, running several possibilities in his head.

"Well, yes, absolutely. This screen is in great condition, obviously having been kept in a stable environment and out of the direct sunlight. If the screen is right, you can probably expect as much as half-a-million dollars or more from the right buyer. There may even be museum interest. Let's see first what I can track down to confirm its provenance."

"That's great. Can you do that for all the objets d'art in this place?"

"Sure. Certainly everything Asian," he added, qualifying his statement. "I brought my digital camera to take images of all of it, and I'll also be taking notes on each one."

He strolled through the room, Doug trailing behind him. Andy loved the first walk through a collection, the anticipation of a marvelous find, the puzzles to solve—especially the puzzles. Who made it? Who commissioned it? Who else owned it? How did it get here?

As he walked, he also picked up a sense of the collector. He enjoyed most those collections that reflected individual tastes. And in truth, every collection held something of the collector. Here, he found that the collector had appreciated whimsy—a carved jade water buffalo whose fat, round belly called out to be tickled, and a twelfth-century ceramic pillow with the Chinese character for "pillow" painted in black glaze in the middle. Andy pointed out the latter to Doug, saying, "Only a Chinese artist would make wordplay of this kind, writing out in the glaze the word for the object itself."

"Yah, and his descendants now sell Irish coffee glasses marked 'Irish Coffee,'" joked Doug.

"Ahhhh! That's who it is. I guess some things never change," replied Andy. They laughed together.

"Go away," he told Doug, "and come back in four to five hours. We'll get something to eat when you come back." Andy turned back to the collection, taking out his digital camera and little notebook while humming to himself.

Hours later, cranky from hunger, he found Doug a welcome sight. He gratefully accepted a sandwich.

"How does it look?"

"This is a terrific collection—he should've died a happy man."

"I think he did. Old age finally got him at ninety-one."

"Okay, I can write up some of the objects right away, like the jade, ivory pieces, and furniture. The Taoist and Buddhist sculptures will take a day or two. A couple of them are Southeast Asian and I will have to check some reference material. Like this—" Andy pointed to a silver-gilded figure standing about a foot-and-a-half high "—is a Maitreya, I think, as listed on the inventory you sent me. It is either the Buddha of the Future or a bodhisattva waiting to become the Buddha of the Future. It is probably from Thailand and I have to check the date, but it could be worth quite a lot. I know an expert in this area, and I may ask her to take a look, too. And as I told you earlier, I'll need to research the screen, which may be the prize of the collection, at least in terms of dollar value. And there is a Chinese painting that looks good and may have good provenance. Let me show you."

Andy led the way back to the library. He stopped before a painting of a couple of small figures in a landscape.

"This," he commented, "is a dated painting by a well-known Ming dynasty artist named Wen Zhengming. He painted at the end of the fifteenth century and into the sixteenth century. Many of these red seals you see on the painting are from collectors, people who owned the painting after the artist finished it. Seals like these tell the story of where the painting has been for the last four hundred years. Most of the seals are from well-known collectors but there are a couple of seals on it that I don't know."

"You mean by another artist?" asked Doug.

Andy shook his head and said a slow, patient "No."

Doug continued, "If it helps, the collector kept records of his purchases and any information about the pieces in these files over here."

"It helps in other ways to have those records, but no, the seals are not related to the artist. Instead, they belong to other collectors, probably from the late nineteenth or early twentieth centuries. I can look them up. I also have to look up the date, just to be as thorough as possible."

Doug frowned. "Will it be hard to trace the seals?"

"Not necessarily," said Andy. "Tracking down the identity of the collectors when you are using just the seals is somewhat complicated, but not impossible. The seal itself does not signify the actual name of the person. Usually, the characters on the seal are a sobriquet, a kind of nickname or studio name, one that the collector chose for himself."

Andy pointed to a small rectangular red seal in the bottom left corner and then to a larger square seal along the left edge of the painting. "These two seals, for example, belong to the same collector. This smaller seal reads in Chinese 'Man of Chaoxian,' and this larger one reads 'Siyuan tang.' The first one actually should be read in Korean as 'Man of Choson,' as in the Choson dynasty in Korea. The collector was a wealthy Korean merchant named An Qi, an avid collector of Chinese art in the first half of the eighteenth century. The other seal is the name of his studio or house. It translates something like the 'Origin of Thoughts Hall.' His seals are a good sign that the painting may be genuine."

"In this case, I recognize the seals, but there are reference materials that, in effect, list the seals and who used them. But keep in mind," Andy cautioned, "that this is not an exact science. Chinese painting is one of the most complicated fields because there are many forgeries—copies of paintings, seals, and signatures. An experienced eye is absolutely necessary, but confirmation through other reproductions and reference materials is equally necessary. Many Western dealers and collectors avoid the field altogether because they are afraid they will be too easily duped. They shouldn't be any more afraid than the Chinese themselves. Many experts are fooled by paintings. It's the nature of the beast."

Andy was quiet for a moment. "To be as sure as possible, I need to do some homework on the major pieces and on the paintings. My reference materials are back in Hong Kong, so it will take some time to put it all together. I'll try to give you recent auction prices for similar pieces where I can."

Doug didn't appear put off by the delay. "I'm waiting on valuations for some real estate and other holdings, so a few weeks shouldn't be a problem. Maybe the delay will cool off the survivors and allow for agreements on who wants what items. I'm preparing for the worst-case scenario, in which the executor uses his discretion to distribute or even sell the items. For that scenario, an accurate appraisal is critical."

"Who is the executor at your firm?" asked Andy.

"Me," admitted Doug, smiling slightly in distaste.

"I'll give it plenty of details and backup, so you'll be on solid ground with the identifications and valuations," assured Andy.

CHAPTER

5

I t was 8:00 a.m. before Andy could get out of bed. The second and third days were always the worst for jetlag. He did his warm-up calisthenics and put on his cross-training shoes. It was a mistake to have skipped his workout the day before. He dragged himself out of the mid-town hotel and jogged north to Central Park. He ran up the west side of Central Park, entering at Seventy-second Street toward the north side of the Boat Pond. Andy headed for the pond's small peninsula, which was framed by two pine trees and a large rock formation. It was tranquil and secluded in the center of the city that never sleeps. Andy was not in the mood for anything too rigorous, and this spot was just right for some gentle taiji. After a few breathing exercises to calm and focus his mind, Andy began the graceful movements associated with the Yang style of taiji. Twenty-five minutes later, Andy finished up and walked out of the park. His mind cleared and body refreshed, Andy had conquered the last of the jet lag.

By late morning, Andy had made his way over to Preston Galleries, also on the Upper East Side. Calvin Preston was an Englishman, originally from Brighton, who ten years earlier had lived in and worked for several dealers in Hong Kong. He and Andy first met at the Cottage House Inn, a pub located in Central, during a darts tournament. Cal fancied himself the local champion and suffered defeat only to the Yank named Andy. A friendship was born, and they had caroused a bit while Cal lived in Hong Kong. A few years ago, Cal moved to New York City to make it on his own as a dealer. In that time, he had turned his business, through some savvy deals, into an up-and-coming auction house. Andy hadn't seen him since Cal's wedding two years earlier.

Cal was seated behind a large mahogany desk. He was tall, angular, and, as always, he looked a bit older than his years. He had a dartboard in his office, and Andy automatically walked toward the board, saying, "Shall we?"

Cal looked up from his desk and smiled. "Not today."

"Yes, I understand. Probably not worth the humiliation," Andy said wryly.

Andy glanced around the sunny office. There was a plush seating area and glass coffee tables piled with auction catalogs. Deftly lighted shelves displayed Cal's impressive collection of carved jades. There were small archaic and zoomorphic figures, primarily Chinese along with a few Incan and Mayan figures. Andy had given Cal a small ring of brown jade in the shape of a pig-dragon, a kind of proto-dragon of the Hongshan peoples of Ancient China, as a token of their friendship. Andy used to wear it around his neck and Cal had coveted it, so Andy made it a parting gift to bring Cal good luck in New York City. Andy smiled when he saw the little piece surrounded by two-dozen more small animals.

"You are doing well, at least by outward appearances," said Andy.

Cal acknowledged the compliment with a nod and quick smile. "Would you like to see my latest treasure?" he asked. Andy nodded, expecting Cal to bring out a new jade. Instead, he spun a silver picture frame on his desk around, revealing a picture of Cal's wife with a new baby.

"That's wonderful," crowed Andy, and Cal beamed. They chatted about family then about mutual friends as they left the gallery and headed for Cal's garaged car. As they headed north on FDR Drive, Andy asked about the collection that Cal would be selling.

"I'm fortunate, or maybe lucky, to have landed this client. I got it through a friend of a friend. The big auction houses are going to envy me this sale, I am sure, but I had to guarantee a minimum price that the sale would bring in."

Andy looked surprised, but only briefly. A contract guaranteeing a minimum sale meant that Cal was on the hook to the owner for that amount, even if the sale brought in less money. The large auction houses eschewed these arrangements, while a smaller house did it sometimes to catch a bigger client.

"I know it's a gamble," agreed Cal, "but I have a good feeling about the collection, and it was assembled with care several generations ago."

"Tell me about the family," prompted Andy.

"The Brookes are a wealthy Connecticut family, WASPy, interested in selling their Asian art collection, because, they say, the items are not to their taste."

Andy snorted. "You mean they aren't as affluent as their predecessors."

Cal shrugged. "I wouldn't be surprised if they just wanted to raise a large sum of money, but I got this sale because a mutual friend suggested I call them. He and the Brookes were at a cocktail party when someone was talking about how hot the Asian art market was, and my friend thought the Brookes looked particularly interested."

Andy nodded. It made perfect sense. The art world was often a small world, and a dealer's connections made all the difference between success or failure. Andy himself was another one of Cal's connections. Andy had worked for Cal in the past to write up Asian objects for his sales catalogues, usually for a flat fee. For a project this large, a collection comprising an entire catalog and auction, Andy would earn a percentage of the sale as well as his expenses. Auction houses produced a catalogue of all the objects for sale, with full-page, color illustrations and detailed descriptions and information—anything that would boost interest and prices. Cal estimated there were almost two hundred Asian objects that were being put up for auction from the Brookes' collection.

"The grandfather, long gone now, was the real collector," explained Cal. "He was a diplomat of some kind in the early 1920s and 1930s, I think posted to China. He was already very wealthy and not shy about buying what he liked while he was in Asia."

"When do we need to be ready?" asked Andy.

"The auction is planned for New York's Asia Week next spring," answered Cal.

Andy nodded. Asia Week was when all the dealers and auction houses held their previews of Asian art, followed by the sales. It was also when the major museums opened their big exhibitions. It happened every spring and fall, a feeding frenzy of collectors, dealers, and museum curators, hosting and attending cocktail parties, lectures, and shows. The huge Armory building on the Upper East Side opened its doors to the public too, with the best of the dealers—by invitation only—showing the cream of their stock for sale. Most important, the serious collectors, the real money, came out for Asia Week.

In about sixty-five minutes they were in Greenwich, an affluent, suburban town that looked very green after the grey hues of Manhattan. The area boasted manicured lawns, rustic piled-rock walls, higher fences with gated drives, and plenty of trees and bushes planted for beauty and privacy. There was a downtown area, with chic shops and food emporiums, but the house they sought was not close to those.

The Brookes' house was on a quiet road, and no houses were even visible from the street. There was a small gatehouse as they turned into the driveway, but the main house was easily another half-mile away from the gateposts.

"They still have plenty of land," commented Andy.

"Yes, but your neighbors would notice if you sold your front yard," suggested Cal.

The house was large and imposing. Its original central section had been built in the late nineteenth century, and two large wings were added in the next. Another pair of smaller stone gateposts announced the house and led to a large cobblestone courtyard. An enormous garage sat off to the left, while open lawns rolled down to the right. The garage still had barn-shaped double doors, several sets of them, and two of the pairs were open to reveal vintage automobiles.

"Nice wheels," smiled Andy.

"Maybe those wheels are part of the reason the Asian collection is up for sale," murmured Cal.

The housekeeper showed them to the living room and Tony Brookes entered soon after. He was in his late forties, dressed in chinos and a polo shirt with a country club insignia over the left breast. Cal introduced Andy, and they all shook hands.

"Andy is here today, Tony, to examine the collection and to take notes for the catalog. The professional photographers will be out later to do their bit. Andy will take his own pictures, but they will be for his reference only. He may need to pick up the pieces, or move them, or open them, in order to identify them. Will that be alright with you?"

"Certainly, of course," Brookes nodded. "Most of the Chinese stuff is in two rooms, a study and a sitting room we've always called the Chinese Room. The housekeeper will show you around and get you anything you need."

The housekeeper reappeared on cue and led them to the sitting room, the so-called Chinese Room. At least they named it something, thought Andy. Late Victorian Chinoiserie wallpaper covered the walls, quasi-Chinese decorative motifs transformed into a baroque style. Virtually everything in the room was in fact Chinese, except the silk-covered Queen Anne furniture, loveseat, sofa, and chairs. It was an opulent room. It looked like it had been used at one time, though less so recently.

"Are we selling the furniture too?" inquired Andy. "The un-upholstered furniture is Chinese and consistent with what a collector would have been able to buy at the turn of the twentieth century. It is primarily late-nineteenth-century Chinoiserie, meaning that the wood is either painted lacquer or painted lacquer with an inlay of hard stones, along with some classic Chinese pieces made from a variety of hardwoods."

"No, not all the furniture, which is a shame, because the two little tables flanking the loveseat look like wonderful folding stools," said Cal.

"They are," agreed Andy, "and probably early Qing dynasty. See those pieces of milky glass decorating the top? It's typical of that period. And they are not shamed by the lamps they support, either. Those lamps, like the stools, are Kangxi period, late-seventeenth century."

Andy walked around the room. "The long table is Chinese, too. See how the ends are turned up? That's so scrolls wouldn't fall off. And it looks like huanghuali wood, a kind of rosewood used for the finest furniture in China," he continued.

They walked over to the table, which held a dozen objects of different media. Andy noted two pairs of tall, five-color, early Qing vases on either end. In between, there were four small gilded-bronze Buddhist figures, probably Qianlong period, eighteenth century from the look of them. In the center sat a large fish jar with a lid, but it was a nineteenth-century copy of a sixteenth-century or Jiajing period piece. Turning, he viewed a set of small cloisonné figures and vessels across the mantel, also from the Qianlong period. After Andy's quick perusal, he was less than excited about the objects in the Chinese Room. The furniture was graceful and quite nice, but the objects, well, they were better than cavorting Hummels but far from rare enough to anchor a catalog. Inside, Andy was dismayed at the deal his friend had made and skeptical about his own fee.

Without changing his expression, Andy said, "Can we see what's in the study?"

"Of course."

They walked through the front foyer through a large living room to a door in the back corner. As soon as Andy walked in, he immediately revised his opinion of Grandpa Brookes. This was the real deal. This space was not so much a study, although there were plenty of bookshelves, as it was a repository of Tang and Sung ceramics and ancient bronzes.

Moments like these were why Andy loved what he did: the thrill of the unexpected find, the charge from encountering something truly spectacular. To view what one artist wrought, at a particular time and place, with whatever training or opportunity, using the materials at hand and ending with a creation beyond words—now that was a great day. This room was filled with such objects, and Andy was filled with a kind of awe and a sense of sharing the artist's moment of passion—and, mixed in with that, a bit of little boy's glee at finding a secret treasure.

There were two walls of art, one of books, and one wall with windows and French doors leading to the gardens beyond. A magnificent double-sided captain's desk sat in front of the books, so that the art lined the walls to the side and the windows to the front. Here is where the man had sat and spent his time.

The housekeeper flipped on the lights and, with a small nod to the men, left the room.

With the lights up, the walls of art became spectacular. The shelves were glass and enclosed in glass, with invisible seams and doors. Each shelf was lit from within, and on one wall was a collection of Chinese bronzes—a collection in and of itself—ranging from the Shang through the Zhou and Han periods. Amazingly, the objects seemed to be arranged chronologically. The opposite wall was the same, but it displayed ceramics, also arranged chronologically, beginning with the early Tang and continuing up to the Northern and then Southern Song periods.

Andy let out a long breath. "These cases are arranged chronologically," Andy said quietly, masking his amazement. He walked over to the bookcases and saw that they were, in fact, filled with books about Chinese art. "And this is an excellent library on Chinese art."

He went back to the art collection, taking notes and muttering to himself. He was utterly absorbed and did not notice when Cal slipped away. Cal returned forty-five minutes later with Tony Brookes.

"Your grandfather arranged his collection in chronological order," repeated Andy admiringly.

"Yes, yes, he was very serious about this business," replied Brookes, waving generally at the room. "Though you'd think that arranging by size or color or something would've made these things more interesting."

Short of crowning Brookes with the closest Shang-period bronze, Andy could think of no reply. Some people didn't deserve the art they had, Andy thought, but this man's indifference to beauty should be a punishable crime. The bronze Andy had selected was a *fangzun*, in Chinese, a large square vase with a sharply flaring lip, about eighteen inches high and wide, with animals decorating the sides and large ram heads coming out of each corner. And it was heavy. Cal must have read Andy's thoughts.

"Tony, where are the scrolls and files?" Cal asked Brookes, changing the subject. Brookes turned to the doors off the side of the bookcases, opening them to reveal a deep closet. Inside, the closet was full, floor to ceiling, with plain and fancy storage boxes, file boxes, maybe, with bills of sale. There was also, at eye level, a set of honeycomb-like shelves. Each little cubbyhole revealed the end of a Chinese scroll or scroll box with a small white hand-written label stuck to it. There were also two wide drawers that appeared to hold fans and album leaves.

Andy said, "Anything in these?"

"I shouldn't think so, it's just paper and the like," said Brookes, "but feel free to have a look. No one has pulled out the scrolls since the old man passed, though he enjoyed hanging them up and switching them about."

"In traditional Chinese households," offered Andy in mild tones, "paintings are displayed according to the time of the year, the season, or the holiday. In an educated family, it would be typical for dozens to rotate during the year."

"If you say so, but it seems a lot of bother to me," responded Brookes, without much interest. Andy eyed the Shang bronze again.

"Is that everything Chinese?" asked Andy quietly. "Are there any more objects that I should know about?"

"No, that's it," replied Cal, turning to Brookes. "Let's leave him to it for a few more minutes."

"Fine. Let me get you a drink." They departed.

Andy selected scrolls at random, hanging the silk loops on the hooks on the wall and gently unrolling each painting. For most, he took photographs, often including the seals and calligraphy, if there were any. Chinese paintings were his passion and he took his time, enjoying the show. An hour had passed quickly by the time Andy closed the closet door.

He found Cal and Tony Brookes in the living room.

"I think Cal should arrange as soon as possible to have everything professionally shot," Andy said. "Are you having Jim and Donna do the work?" Andy asked Cal, naming the best photography team he knew. They were expensive but produced knock-out pictures, even of junkyard dogs. Their pictures would stand out, which was important in the flood of materials produced for each Asia Week.

"Probably. I mentioned the job to them and have to firm up the dates to do the work. We may get lucky and catch them between jobs now," said Cal.

"They are the best around," Cal added for Tony Brookes.

"Fine, fine," Brookes said.

"Cal tells me that your grandfather also left diaries covering his time in China, when he probably bought the bulk of the collection. I'd like to see them, if you don't mind. That kind of detail in a catalog makes for a nice introduction and, depending on the stories, may add some cachet to some of the pieces," said Andy.

"I'll have copies made for you," agreed Brookes.

* * * *

Andy was quiet when they started their drive back to the City. Cal let him think for a few minutes then teased, "Which object did you want to hit him with?"

"Oh," Andy exhaled, "one of the really heavy bronzes."

"Not the big plates?" laughed Cal.

"Oh no, not on that hard head," Andy retorted. After another pause, he added, "Collectors come in all shapes and sizes. Some collect just one medium or just one period or just one color. Brookes senior collected Chinese art very systematically and very thoroughly for the time."

"What did you think of it?" demanded Cal at last.

"By all means, let's find it a new owner or two. It's a first-rate collection, so you have several options. The pieces in the Chinese Room are nice examples of their kind and will be attractive to beginning collectors or to people who just want pretty things in their homes. The walls in the study have very good to excellent pieces, and the scrolls may be equally valuable. I'm surprised that no one knew about this collection."

"Apparently the grandfather was a very private man, even after his retirement from the diplomatic corps. Hopefully we'll learn more about him from his memoirs, but he seemed to have collected for his own pleasure, not for other people," added Cal.

"Well, you can do several catalogues, one each for the bronzes, the ceramics, the paintings, and the other miscellaneous objects. They can all be in one publication or four separate ones. If you are able to include some of the furniture from the Chinese Room, you may do better with the decorative pieces. I think you can sell the collections as whole lots without breaking them up, and I know at least a half-a-dozen collectors who would be interested in the paintings and the ceramics. There are two youngish collectors I know in Hong Kong who would definitely be interested."

"Do you really think I should try first to sell them as entire lots?"

"No question. You always have the option of breaking up the collection and selling it piecemeal. Let's get them photographed as soon as possible. Please remind Jim to give me detailed shots of all the seals and inscriptions on the paintings and any inscriptions in the bronzes. Then I can start to work on writing. I'll give you some estimates on value too, especially if you want to try to sell the specific collections."

"Do you want to see them again?" asked Cal.

"I will come back once you have them all in your warehouse for the final look before we send the text to press. You got yourself a winner here. Good for you, Cal."

Cal was pleased by the praise and the prospects. They parted cordially, each engrossed in his own thoughts.

* * * *

Andy was tired. It was hard work to absorb so many objects in such a short time. When Andy got up to his room, the message light on the hotel telephone was blinking. Andy had charged his mobile phone battery but had turned it off while examining the Brookes collection. Andy felt a sick, heavy feeling as he pushed the message button. It was Chen Wenbeng, calling to say Sifu was dangerously ill and that Andy needed to call his friends in Hong Kong. Andy's sick feeling spread up his throat and he had to remind himself to swallow.

Then he turned his mobile phone back on. Yes, there was another message, this one from Danny Chung, telling him to come home. Chen Wenbeng had called to say that Sifu was seriously ill. Danny had called with the same message. Andy considered his options. He had seen both collections and could do the next stage of writing from any location. He could return home even that night, if he could get a seat. He made his arrangements with the airline and called both Doug and Cal about the change in plans. With his digital pictures, notes, and fresh memories of the items, he would be able to start work.

CHAPTER
6

ndy made the next flight, though he barely had time to stuff his pockets with Twizzlers before he had to board. On the plane again, Andy had time to think. He took calming breaths, assuring himself that Sifu would be fine, as though Andy had the power to cure him simply by showing up. Andy knew it would sound strange to his American colleagues if he told them he needed to return to Hong Kong to attend to his sick martial arts teacher. Instead, he'd told them that he had seen enough and was ready to start.

Few people outside of the martial arts understood the relationship between a martial arts teacher and his best or favorite students. The martial arts teacher-student relationship was based on an oral teaching tradition built over time—a long period of time. The idea of tradition, especially in a Chinese context, was about time in terms of tens of generations, rather than a linear, Western sense of time. Martial arts training, unlike the academic year, never ended, and training with a martial arts teacher—or *sifu* in Cantonese, the language spoken in Hong Kong—was about a long-term relationship. The relationship covered far more than the physical training, because a sifu also had the responsibility of setting moral and spiritual guidelines for the student, of providing the framework that prepared the student for life and all its changes. The bond formed was sometimes unbreakable, often stronger than that between parent and child.

Andy considered the common martial arts expression: "There are no bad students only bad teachers." In China, a high expectation was placed on teachers and scholars, but in return, the Chinese revered and honored their teachers.

As with many teacher-student relationships, over time, a small number of students stayed the course, continuing to advance. Some students had the talent and the determination to become the next generation of teachers. These students often become the lieutenants of the teacher, teaching the younger students and acting as a kind of honor guard. They set the standards for the younger students and they carried prestige within the martial arts system that their teacher had created. Andy was such a high-ranking student, and he shared a bond as well with the other similarly ranked students. In many ways, the four of them comprised Sifu's family. His wife had passed away about ten years ago and his son had been killed by a high fever as a small boy in the late 1960s. Andy was completely lost in thoughts of his teacher as he faded to sleep.

* * * *

As soon as Andy got back on the ground, he called Danny Chung for an update.

"I'm back," he said to Danny. "How is he?"

"He's in the hospital in Kowloon," answered Danny. "No one knows what the problem is. It may be food poisoning, and the white coats just want to run more tests."

"This is baffling to me. He didn't look sick when I left, just a little tired maybe."

Danny's voice was steady, reassuring. "His *qi* is so strong, he probably ignored all the symptoms," commented Danny.

"How are these doctors? Is Sifu even speaking to them? Where is Dr. Yip?" For a moment, Andy's fears got away from him. Dr. Yip was Sifu's traditional Chinese doctor, one who diagnosed by reading pulses and checking physiognomy, taking only minutes to locate the source of the problem.

"Dr. Yip is on the mainland again, gathering various plants and other materials for his herbal treatments. He hasn't seen Sifu yet. We are still trying to track him down."

Andy sighed, understanding that Yip could be wandering somewhere in some hills and that it could take days, even weeks, to find him. China was a big place to look for someone. Then it occurred to Andy that Dr. Yip would suddenly appear, "knowing" he was needed.

"He wants to see you, by the way, as soon as you can get there," added Danny. Andy assured Danny he'd be on his way within minutes, and they hung up.

Andy took a quick shower and headed over to Kowloon, across the harbor from Wanchai. He was in a hurry, so he skipped the cheap but slower ferry and used a cab to go through the Harbor Tunnel. He found Peter Tsui in the hospital hallway and gave him a brief greeting before entering the hospital room. "He is barely conscious," Peter warned, "and very weak."

Andy bowed slightly as he entered his room, showing the traditional sign of respect. He then stepped farther into the room. "Sifu, I bring you greetings from your cousin in New York, Chen Wenbeng, and the wish for a speedy recovery."

Sifu lay on the bed, looking smaller and quieter than Andy had ever seen him. His eyes opened at the sound of Andy's voice, but he did not try to speak.

"Sifu, what can I do for you?" It was hard for Andy to see his teacher looking pale and weak. He only knew him as a robust personality. Normally thin, he was wiry and limber, usually strong and capable of manifesting tremendous amounts of *qi*. Today, he looked diminished, sapped.

"Do you remember when my brother died?" he whispered.

"Of course, Sifu. I was at the funeral." Andy could not have been more astonished at the question.

"His painting," Sifu tried again, but he ran out of energy.

"Yes, I remember, Sifu. You wanted me to help you with it when I got back. Just tell me what to do."

"Special," started Sifu, working hard to keep speaking. "Ni Zan."

Special was an understatement. Ni Zan was a Yuan dynasty master. Extraordinary was more like it, thought Andy.

"Okay, your brother gave you a Ni Zan painting before he died," filled in Andy.

Sifu nodded, closing his eyes for a moment.

"Help me," a pause. "Fix it," he whispered, without opening his eyes.

Andy waited, but Sifu said no more. His chest rose and fell, but he did not try to speak again. Andy waited another minute, then bowed and left the room. Peter was waiting outside and Andy was glad.

"He spoke of his brother's death, or his funeral to be exact," said Andy. Peter looked blank.

"You remember, you were there too," insisted Andy. Peter nodded.

"Was there anything odd about it?" asked Andy.

"Not that I noticed, nothing out of place except you, the only blue-eyed mourner," noted Peter.

Andy trusted Peter's instincts. Peter worked for the Hong Kong police, not as an officer, but as a computer troubleshooter. He had worked for more than ten years for half-a-dozen investment banking firms but found more satisfaction working for the police. He made sure that no one hacked into the Hong Kong police computer systems, and he often helped to track computer crimes. He was a quiet man, with the fastest hands Andy had ever seen. Peter tended to carry a variety of knives. They were Peter's weapon of choice and, given the speed he moved, they were all he would ever need. Peter was an excellent chef, too, feeding his entire family. He lived with his parents, a brother and sister-in-law and their two kids, real Chinese style. His mother avoided the kitchen when Peter was cooking—not Chinese style at all—because the speed with which the knives flew around the counter scared her to death.

"Apparently, his brother left him a painting and he wants me to fix it," said Andy.

"What's wrong with it?" asked Peter.

"He didn't say," replied Andy. It might have been that Sifu was too weak to continue. It might have been that Sifu was a man of few words.

Chen Xiaohu was a man steeped in classic Chinese traditions, in which actions spoke louder than words. He was the elder son of a Chinese general, and he'd received an excellent education as the son of a respected, high-ranking army official. Xiaohu even studied in America, where he obtained a post-graduate degree from Yale and a lifelong fondness for red Fireball candy. He returned to China and taught Classics at Beijing Daxue, Beijing University or Beida for short, and then at University of Hong Kong when he moved to the New Territories. Along the way, he mastered several forms of martial arts, including tai chi, Yang style. He was the ideal teacher, blending the intellectual, spiritual, and physical.

In many ways, it was typical for Sifu to give Andy a task, to "fix" the painting, but then to let Andy sort out what needed to be fixed and the right way to do so. Actions spoke louder than words.

Andy also felt honored by the task because it involved Sifu's family, and Sifu took the honor of his family very seriously.

Returning to the moment, Andy said, "So what's the deal here? I haven't been away for a week and this is not good."

"It happened the day after you left, also the day that Dr. Yip left for the mainland."

"Are you on top of getting Dr. Yip here as soon as he steps off the plane?" Andy asked.

"Yes. I just got a message that he is on his way. I hope to see him as early as tomorrow morning," replied Peter.

"Have you talked to Sifu's nephew?" was Andy's next question.

"No, the Little Turtle's Egg has not even come by."

Peter and Andy were in agreement about Chen Ding, meaning that both were inclined to dislike him. After his father's death, Chen Ding was quick to return to work, a real estate business he had started with his father's limited backing. It was disrespectful for Ding to fail to mourn his father properly, and it dishonored the Chen family. Andy and Peter, as well as Danny and Tommy, felt the slight to the Chen family as keenly as Xiaohu.

Andy waited for the answer to the next obvious question, and Peter replied, "Yes, he has been told. Tommy tracked him down and left a message."

Tommy was the managing agent for a huge real estate business and could find anyone in the business. In many ways, Hong Kong was too small a town for anyone not to know everyone in his or her field.

"What's with that? What kind of filial piety is that?" Andy demanded, referring to the Confucian ethical principle whereby all relatives take care of their family members and show the proper respect. The tradition of respect went beyond the living, as Sifu's concern about his obligation to take care of the painting given him by his brother showed.

"I don't think any of us like him," Peter shrugged. "He fancies himself a modern man, which I take to mean that he does not consider himself Chinese."

"Well, alright," Andy sighed. "Keep me posted if anything changes."

He knew that he had been given the rare opportunity to work with objects that had long been off the map of the Chinese art world, and that was exciting. His excitement was tempered by his worry about Sifu.

CHAPTER
7

arly the next morning, Andy took the ferry to Lantau for his workout. It felt important that he work out on the plateau. In his gym bag, he had several smooth and flattened river and beach stones, about twice the size of his fist and weighing a pound or two each.

Andy had been struggling with a set of exercises in which every part of the body was in constant motion. The exercise required a sudden mini-explosion of energy, telescoping into a single hand or foot movement. There was a split second where nothing moved, a kind of frozen moment, and this focus generated an extremely powerful and explosive energy. Andy's stone collection, gathered from riverbeds and beaches, was for "breaking" practice. These stones had been pounded for thousands, possibly millions, of years, and thus were rendered particularly hard. If hit with the proper kind of high-energy strike, the kind Andy had been trying to develop, the stone would explode. He had seen Sifu do it any number of times in private lessons and public demonstrations, holding a stone in one hand and smacking the stone with the opposite hand. Once, in a public show, Sifu held a large stone in each hand and smacked them both to his forehead one after another. The stones exploded and the applause was thunderous. To his students, it was a pointed lesson that the energy could be manifested on any part of the body.

Andy had only cracked the stones so far, never achieving the explosion of the well-executed technique. Of course, cracking the stones was an accomplishment, just not the one that Andy sought. Mastering this skill would make his striking techniques more powerful. Learning to master it was also part of the discipline. And it made him nuts that he couldn't do it yet.

Today, after an hour's practice, Andy still could not do more than crack the stones. It was the kind of thing that might take years to perfect and would not "work" until it was perfectly executed.

* * * *

Back at Central, Andy quickly showered and changed clothes. He checked his watch and noted that his haste had paid off with some extra time. He placed a call to Yoshio Shubazaki, a Japanese investment banker and serious collector of Japanese screens. Yoshio was an exceptional collector, in part because he remembered every screen he ever saw. He also had an excellent private library on the topic. Andy thought Yoshio would be helpful in identifying the screen in the estate collection. Yoshio agreed to see him that morning.

It was a quick cab ride to Yoshio's apartment, which was in Mid-level, the apartments above Central on the Hong Kong side. Yoshio lived on the top floor of an apartment on Garden Road, with a spectacular view of Hong Kong Harbor. Yoshio was a creature of habit, leaving his building every morning at 8:50 a.m. sharp to arrive at his office at 9 a.m. sharp. Yoshio's driver always got it exactly right. "Ahhh, Japanese precision," Andy said aloud to himself, as he alighted at the building.

Yoshio was pleased to see Andy. They addressed each other using quasi-Japanese honorifics. In Japan, the usual honorific is to add "san" to the last name, such as Shubazaki-san. Andy and

Yoshio varied the honorific by adding "san" to their first names, joining the formality of Japan with the more casual American mode.

"Yoshio-san, o-hio go zai mas. O genki des ka?" Andy said, asking: "Good morning and how are you?"

"Andy-san, o-hio, o-hio. Genki. Anata wa?" Yoshio returned the good morning, responded that he was fine, and asked how Andy was doing.

"Genki, genki." Fine, fine.

"Andy-san, I hear your sensei is in the hospital," Yoshio said seriously, using the Japanese word for teacher. "I hope it is nothing too serious."

"Yoshio-san, I am always amazed at how small a town Hong Kong can be," Andy said. Curious, he asked, "How did you hear?"

"That's what makes this city work—knowledge. And, of course, money," Yoshio responded, non-committal. Andy understood this answer. Even if he and Yoshio were blood brothers, Yoshio might never tell him how he had found out. Yoshio dispensed information in the most complex of ways. And, as much as Yoshio liked Andy, Andy was still not family, and thus it would be futile to ask again.

"I'll know more about my Sensei's condition later this morning," Andy said. "In the meantime, I have a screen I would like you to look at." Andy opened the briefcase he carried and pulled out the color print he had made that morning. He handed it to Yoshio.

Yoshio sucked in some air and let out a "hmmm" kind of sound.

"It's a single screen in a private collection in New York," explained Andy, "and I want to know if it has a mate—it looks like it is part of a set. I thought you might recognize it. The seals and signature appear genuine, as far as I can tell. And," Andy paused, "it's in mint condition."

"Interesting," was Yoshio's only response. Yoshio was hooked. Andy smiled to himself.

"I can leave this picture with you, and you can think about it. Just let me know. It may be for sale out of an estate."

Andy tossed in the last comment as extra incentive. He checked his watch. It was 8:30. Yoshio escorted him to the door, and they traded farewells. By the time Andy reached the lobby, there was a cab waiting for him. "An efficient man," Andy smiled, again to himself.

* * * *

On the way to Kowloon, Andy checked his cell phone and found a message from Peter. Dr. Yip had been located and was arriving at the airport in about an hour. Just as he started to put the mobile phone away, it rang.

"Yes, there is a mate to the screen," confirmed Yoshio. "First, I want to know if I can have rights of first refusal should it become available for sale."

"I am sure that it can be arranged," agreed Andy, thinking that there was always room for a negotiation. "I know the lawyer for the family."

"If it is indeed genuine, the other half belongs to Boston."

"The Museum of Arts?" Andy asked.

"Yes," Yoshio said.

"I bet they'd love to get their hands on it," countered Andy. "It seems a shame not to reunite them."

"They would not be able to afford it right now, I am told," Yoshio told him blandly, "and I might be willing to let them borrow it now and then."

Andy knew he would try to broker the deal for Yoshio to obtain the screen. It would be worth it on several levels. Andy

would earn a fee for a successful deal and, maybe more importantly, Yoshio would be indebted to him, which was a more
valuable currency.

"Is it reproduced anywhere?" Andy asked, seeming to
change the subject.

"Boston's half was in Kyoto last year at the National Museum.
It's in the catalogue," Yoshio answered.

"Okay, thanks. I'll check it out and let you know about the
authenticity, after I tell my client. I'll be in touch."

"Yes, soon." And Yoshio hung up.

Andy shook his head. Yoshio had known right away that
there was another half to the screen and never let on. He made a
note to himself to email Doug later and let him know he had a
buyer in the wings—well, more like on center stage.

* * * *

Andy was the first to arrive at Sifu's hospital room. As always, he
bowed slightly upon entering the room. Andy was a little surprised
that he had beaten them, given that Ah Pun, Tommy's regular
driver, was at the wheel.

Ah Pun had once stolen cars for a living in Hong Kong. In the
early 1990s, he was a member of a gang of teenagers who stole
Mercedes Benzes in Hong Kong and drove them to armored
speedboats, which transported them to the mainland for sale on
the black market. It was easy money for a short time. There was no
long-term future in it, however, because only cheap leaded fuel
was available in the mainland. All those finely crafted, deluxe
German engines that ran on unleaded fuel would seize up, and
there was no place to repair them. Ah Pun got busted at the harbor
slip in Aberdeen. Ah Pun was some kind of cousin to Peter, and
Peter's connections through the police department helped Ah Pun
get a lighter sentence. On his release, Peter got him a legitimate

wheel job, one that allowed him to report to his parole officer. Tommy had needed a new driver. And everyone had a driver in Hong Kong. Tommy suspected Ah Pun had other skills, but he had yet to call upon them.

"Sifu," Andy said by way of greeting, "I went out to Lantau for a workout this morning."

Sifu opened his eyes and nodded. "What are you working on?" he asked softly.

"I'm still trying to do high-energy breaks on beach stones," Andy answered. He was relieved to see that Sifu was lucid and apparently no weaker than the day before.

"Hmm." Sifu was silent, perhaps thinking about something.

"Danny tells me that Dr. Yip will be here pretty soon," said Andy.

"Did you bring one? A stone? Let me see you break it now," Sifu said, ignoring the other comment.

Andy knew better than to wonder how Sifu knew he still had stones in his briefcase. He just did. Andy reached into his bag and took one out. Andy placed the stone on the bed and began a series of movements to warm up and get into the particular mind set. It was a waste of time to do it cold. Sifu watched carefully. Andy stood at the side of the bed and, after about a minute, he picked up the stone and hit it. There was a loud smacking sound but the stone just sat there, mocking him.

"Don't drop your shoulder. There can be no extra motion. Try it again. Remember, store power like drawing a bow, issue power like shooting an arrow."

Andy performed another set of hand motions to help raise the *qi* and focus his mind. He picked up the stone and adjusted his motion as he hit it. The stone exploded into a dozen pieces. Andy looked shocked for a moment.

"Sometimes it is only the slightest of mistakes. Something so minor you are barely aware of it yourself. But once corrected, the technique is flawless and thus you achieve the desired results," Sifu said calmly. He sat back and closed his eyes, tired from the slight exertion.

Andy looked at the pieces of stone littering the floor and nodded his head in understanding. "Thank you," he replied. "I have been working on this technique for some time."

"And now you have mastered it. Keep practicing," came Sifu's soft reply.

Peter walked in with Dr. Yip and Tommy close behind. Peter and Tommy paused to bow. Peter looked at Andy and Sifu and then down at the mess on the floor. He snorted, saying, "This is a hospital, not a work out hall!"

Tommy craned his neck to see. "A private lesson, eh?"

The martial arts brothers laughed. Dr. Yip smiled, too, glad that his patient was well enough to be teaching.

Tommy said, "I am glad you finally got that technique down. Now you can start whining about something else."

The light mood turned more serious when Dr. Yip sat next to Sifu and took his wrist to feel the pulses. Dr. Yip moved his fingers slightly on Sifu's wrist, occasionally checking facial features to confirm his impressions. He was quiet, concentrating.

Aware this could take some time, Andy found a broom and swept up the stone shards on the floor lest the nurse come in and throw the whole lot of them out.

Finally, Dr. Yip leaned back in the chair and announced, "This is serious."

The three students stood around the bed and looked at each other, then at Sifu, then back to Dr. Yip. Dr. Yip was talking to Sifu. "You have a toxin in your bloodstream. It has been there for quite

some time. I am surprised that I did not pick up on it before. It must have been such a small quantity at first. It seems to have affected the liver and the heart. This is not good. Perhaps a recent catalyst was introduced that magnified the speed of its degenerative progress. Most interesting. I must return to my studio and look up these symptoms to get a more accurate diagnosis…"
Dr. Yip trailed off, lost in thought.

"Ah Pun can take you," offered Tommy. "As we can't use our mobile phones in here, I'll call him from the nurse's station and have him meet you at the front door." He left to find the phone.

"What should we do?" Andy asked Dr. Yip.

"You must bring him to my studio. He must leave here. They can do nothing for him here."

"Now? Can we just walk out? Just like that?" Andy asked. But Peter was already out the door, looking for the doctors or nurses who were necessary to do just that.

Moments later, Peter returned with a young doctor in tow. The doctor protested, "It is not as simple as saying that you want to leave. You must get permission."

Tommy returned, too. "Let's make that happen, shall we?" he asked. "You're a doctor, you make it happen."

Peter added, "Do not think for a moment that we are not serious. We are leaving with this man, with or without the hospital's permission."

"He must be released by his physician," protested the doctor again, but with less heart this time.

"That's easy," Andy spoke up. "This is Dr. Yip. This is his physician." Andy gestured to Dr. Yip.

The young doctor looked at the tiny, wizened figure that was Dr. Yip. Dr. Yip nodded in response, saying, "What these young men say is in fact true. This is my patient. And I am his doctor. I have been since his birth."

"Wow!" Andy thought. He knew Dr. Yip was old, but this put a little perspective on the date. Dr. Yip had to be, like, ninety years old.

"I see," said the much younger doctor. He took up the chart placed in the door and studied it. He said, "This is against my recommendation. We do not know the source of the problem here. And I cannot in good faith release him unless I am satisfied that he will get the treatment he needs." The young doctor started to puff up slightly as he said all this.

Andy, Tommy, and Peter all moved a step closer to the young doctor, hemming him in. His bravado immediately dissipated. "On the other hand," he added quickly, looking at Dr. Yip, "as his primary physician, I am sure you are more qualified and more familiar with the patient's personal history, and given your obvious years of experience, Dr. Yip, I am sure that we can release him into your care immediately."

"Good answer," said Peter.

"But he must leave the building in a wheelchair. That's mandatory hospital policy," the young doctor said, mustering up a little dignity and exerting the only authority he had left.

"No problem," agreed Andy, Peter, and Tommy simultaneously.

Ten minutes later, Sifu was dressed and rolling out the front door. Ah Pun waited at the door to Tommy's car. Ah Pun drove Sifu, Dr. Yip, and Tommy to Dr. Yip's studio. Tommy would call when there was news. Andy called Danny's mobile and left an update, then headed back to his apartment while Peter headed to his office.

* * * *

Andy arrived back home in time for lunch, and he then returned to work. He turned on his computer and abandoned it in the next moment. Feeling like he was in the wrong place, Andy called over to Dr. Yip's apartment for an update—or so he thought. But when Dr. Yip answered the phone, Andy invited himself over and Dr. Yip agreed.

Causeway Bay, where Dr. Yip lived, was a stone's throw from Wanchai in linear distance, but a hundred year's away in appearance. It was an older part of Hong Kong Island, with narrower streets, older buildings, and far less incursion of Western styles. Dr. Yip lived among the other apothecaries and herbalists.

Andy bowed to Dr. Yip as he entered the studio, according him the respect due an older, learned man. "What have you concluded?" he asked.

"Your Sifu is resting quietly in the other room," said Dr. Yip solemnly. "It is very serious. He has ingested a toxin that remains in his body. It is slowly draining him of his strength, which is a remarkable thing considering the man. The toxin is both complex and quite subtle. And it is no accident."

"What do we need to do for him?" asked Andy.

"He is resting now, a good thing, but I fear that I may not be able to save him. I am trying to cleanse his system," Dr. Yip responded.

"What do you mean?" Andy anxiously asked.

"We don't know what the toxin is, so we cannot combat it directly. In the meantime, he will continue to weaken. If we knew what he had consumed in the past few months, it might provide some clues. But the difficulty is, he has already digested those things. I asked if he had changed anything in his diet and he said he could not think of anything." Dr. Yip put his ancient forefinger to his wisp of a beard and thought for a moment. "Perhaps there is something in his apartment that can help us." He looked at Andy expectantly.

"Sure, let's go immediately. Can we leave Sifu alone?" Andy said.

"My wife is here," Dr. Yip said. Andy called Tommy and minutes later, Ah Pun pulled up with the car.

* * * *

Thirty-five minutes later, they were back in Lantau, unlocking Sifu's apartment. Lantau was accessible by a bridge and highway that had been added for the new airport. Andy had a key, as did all the other high-ranking students, and he let himself and Dr. Yip in. The apartment was simply furnished, with wide windows to let in the light. Andy let Dr. Yip enter first. Dr. Yip would be searching for anything out of the ordinary, a sound, a smell, a change in the way the space felt.

Andy followed Dr. Yip on his tour through the apartment. Dr. Yip walked through the small foyer into the living room. He went through the bedroom, out onto the balcony, and then into the bathroom and the study. Finally, he went through the swinging door that led into the kitchen, where he stopped just inside the door and stood silently turning his head, looking and listening carefully. He slowly walked around the kitchen, lingering near the counter tops. Dr. Yip opened a few cabinet doors, then the refrigerator. Suddenly, he turned to Andy and said, "I think it is here. Can you leave this room for a few minutes? Perhaps wait for me in the living room."

Andy quietly left the kitchen. He understood that any other presence besides Dr. Yip's in the kitchen would be a distraction. Andy went to the living room but then moved on to the study. He glanced at the desk in passing and noted the wooden scroll box, with an inscription on the lid in Chinese characters. He looked more closely at the inscription; the words "Ni yuanzhen jiu ting tu" were followed by two characters that read "shenpin."

He nodded to himself, thinking this must be the painting that Sifu had mentioned. Translated, the title read, "The Autumn

Pavilion painted by Yuanzhen." Yuanzhen was the painter Ni Zan's fancy or style name. "Shenpin" meant "divine object," which was the highest rank in traditional Chinese painting. Whoever wrote the inscription felt that the painting was an extraordinary piece. Andy was curious about the appellation of "divine object" and wondered who might have added it.

He opened the box and removed the silk wrapping around the rolled-up scroll. Then Andy untied the string that kept the painting from unrolling, taking care as he opened the scroll. The mounting was in very good shape, so he could hang it by the string at the top of the mounting. Sifu had several hooks on his wall for hanging scrolls. Andy found an empty one on the wall immediately to left of the desk that appeared to be the right size to hang the entire painting.

He glanced about for the painting hanger, a three-foot piece of bamboo with a little iron hook at the end, specifically made to set hanging scrolls on the wall. These hangers could be used in two ways. A painting could be viewed upright in its entirety, by hooking the string at the top and unrolling the painting with one hand while holding the stick with the other, or, the painting could be hooked using the stick to place the string on a hook or nail on the wall. The painting then simply unrolled down the wall. Andy used the bamboo stick to hang the painting on the wall and unrolled it gently.

He saw the inscription first and then the painting in its entirety. It was fantastic.

"Waaah! This is an amazing painting," he exclaimed out loud. It measured about two-and-a-half feet high and maybe eighteen inches wide. It was a simple landscape painting, an ink monochrome on paper, meaning there were no other colors but the ink itself. In the foreground at the bottom right was a little spit of land with four tall, mostly leafless trees. At the base of the trees was a simple structure of four posts and a thatched roof, obviously the "Autumn Pavilion" referred to in the title. In the middle to distant ground, there was a set of low, simply-drawn hills made with a greyish wash and dark black texture dots. At the very top on the right, there was an inscription followed by the signature and seal of the artist.

Everything about the painting was typical of Ni Zan's *pingdan* style. Often translated as "plain" or "insipid" style, it was distinguished by a very narrow range of ink tones and simple visual compositions, only the most minimal of everything. Even the simple pavilion featured in this one was typical.

This example had a number of collector's seals, which ran around the edge of the painting, particularly down the right edge. If this was a genuine painting of the fourteenth century by Ni Zan, the large number of seals would be appropriate. Examining it closely, Andy noticed minute foxing, a bloom of rust colored dots, in the top left corner—was this the problem that Sifu had recognized? Considering the age of the painting, a small amount of foxing was not surprising. The painting itself was mounted on several layers of paper, a process that protected the painting from light and moisture. The little patch of foxing meant that mold and moisture had penetrated that area. Although expensive to do properly, it was possible to fix this problem. Andy began taking pictures, including close-ups of the seals and the artist's signature. When he put away his camera and stood still, admiring the painting, Dr. Yip came into the study.

"Have you seen this?" Andy asked, pointing to the painting on the wall.

Dr. Yip walked up to the painting, looked it up and down, and pronounced it "a very nice Ni Zan painting." Smiling slightly at Andy's surprise, Dr. Yip turned and said matter-of-factly, "I think I have found the source of the problem with your teacher."

Andy said, "Okay, let me put this back in its box and I'll be there in a second." Andy muttered slightly to himself. Why should he be surprised that Dr. Yip was knowledgeable about Chinese paintings? The man was a day older than water and had had time to learn many things. Andy began to roll up the scroll, and when he could not comfortably stretch any higher, he reached down for the painting hanger and unhooked the painting. He turned the painting upside down and finished rolling. He then tied the string loosely around the scroll, so as not to damage the mounting. Andy wrapped the painting in the silk wrapper and returned it to the box. All the while, Dr. Yip stood patiently watching him. Andy grabbed his camera and they headed toward the kitchen. Andy waited as Dr. Yip preceded him through the swinging door.

Dr. Yip walked over to the dish drain and said, "There is some residue on your teacher's teacup. We will take this."

Andy considered asking Dr. Yip how he knew there was residue on the cup. Sanity prevailed, however, and he refrained. Dr. Yip would doubtless reply with an answer that did not answer anything he had asked. Elder even to Sifu, Dr. Yip was entitled to answer questions with questions—the Greek's Socratic method of teaching had nothing on the Chinese—but Andy did not feel the need to seek out a lesson. He accepted that Dr. Yip just knew the cup had residue. As Dr. Yip began to reach for the cup, Andy said, "Please," and proceeded to take a picture of the scene before anything was moved. They were hardly forensic scientists, but it would be a record.

Dr. Yip wrapped the blue and white teacup with its lid in a plastic zip-locked baggie. This was actually fairly scientific so Andy did not complain.

"I also believe that one of these teas is the source," stated Yip. He walked over to the kitchen cabinet, opened the door, and pointed to four square tin cans of tea. This time, he stood aside and Andy took more pictures. Each tin had a different kind of tea written on the side: Dragon Well, Black Dragon, Jasmine, and Green teas. Dr. Yip took all four cans and placed them in another, larger plastic bag.

"You can do your tests and we can also have Peter send samples to the police lab for analysis. Someone should be able to tell us if there is anything unusual," Andy said, as they closed up the apartment behind them.

On the quick drive back to Causeway Bay, Andy said to Dr. Yip, "In the hospital, Sifu mentioned that he felt surrounded by evil."

Dr. Yip nodded.

Andy continued, "He seemed to think it started just before his brother died last year."

Dr. Yip nodded again, storing the information away with the other seemingly stray facts.

Back at the studio, Andy called Peter about their speculations. Peter agreed to come by and collect the samples for testing. Andy called Tommy and Danny, too, to give them updates. Danny promised to come by the studio and sit with Sifu that evening.

ndy headed to Victoria Park the next morning for his workout. On the spur of the moment, he hopped the high-speed ferry to Lantau and headed to the reservoir. He was soon joined by Peter, Danny, and Tommy, all without prior arrangement.

Each performed his own series of warm-up exercises. Then, after a brief consultation, they agreed on and went through a series of choreographed martial arts forms. By the end of the first form, they were all moving in unison, as one. They performed the rest of the workout together, finding comfort in each other's presence. Finally, they decided to work on a special form that Sifu had designed. They had only just learned it in the last few months and much of its subtleties they had not yet discussed with their teacher. They decided to work out their questions on their own, and between the four of them, they were successful.

"Sifu will be surprised," said Andy.

"So you think so, little brother?" asked Tommy gently. "Are we not masters?"

Andy smiled in response. Sometimes he forgot.

"I spoke with Dr. Yip last night," said Danny. "He asked me to stop by Sifu's apartment this morning and pick up some objects that reflect the quality of Sifu's *qi*. Who will join me?"

Danny was the quietest of the group, almost taciturn. He was very deliberate in his martial arts, as well. Very exacting in his dealings, he did well in the import-export business.

"I'll go with you," offered Andy.

"I picked up the samples at Yip's and brought them to the lab. This isn't a police investigation, strictly interpreted, but it might become one, depending on what we learn," said Peter quietly.

"Sifu mentioned to me that he felt an evil presence in the shadows of his life, as early as last year when his brother died," Andy told his friends. They nodded in understanding.

"What did his brother die from?" asked Danny.

"I think it was a heart attack," said Andy. "He had a diet from hell, all those fried foods."

Danny drove them to Sifu's apartment. This time when Andy entered, the air seemed stale and the apartment hollow. Danny wandered about, trying to select items. Andy picked up one of Sifu's swords. He made cuts through the air, feeling the balance and weight of the sword. He also felt Sifu's presence and traces of his *qi* in the handle and when he swung the blade. He placed the sword in a sword bag that had a shoulder strap, choosing to bring it to Dr. Yip's. Danny brought in Sifu's calligraphy brushes and one of his official robes. Andy added those to his gym bag. Andy noticed the scroll box with the Ni Zan painting, and after a moment's thought, decided to place that in his bag as well.

They swung open the door to leave and came face-to-face with Sifu's nephew. He had a key in his outstretched hand.

"Chen Ding, what do you want?" asked Danny in astonishment.

He scowled in response. "It is better for you to tell me what you are doing here. I hope you are not disturbing my uncle's things."

"We came by to water the plants," lied Andy glibly. Danny turned to look at him.

"How did you get in?" demanded Chen Ding.

"Sifu gave us both keys years ago," replied Danny quietly, "but I did not know that he gave one to you."

"I have my uncle's key. I am family," replied Ding, playing the Chinese trump card. He looked down at Andy's full bag. "What have you stuffed in there?"

"We are on our way out now, as you can see. This is my work out bag," he said, holding out his gym bag. "Do you want to check it?"

Chen Ding looked tempted but shook his head. He said, "I can look after things now, you needn't come by any more." This was said with growing confidence as he realized that Danny and Andy would not challenge him.

Danny started to respond but Andy cut him off, saying mildly, "Okay, thanks. We'll be sure to tell Sifu you are looking after things here. I am sure he will be pleased."

The two made it down to the parking lot before Danny demanded an explanation. "What was that all about? We had every good reason to be in that apartment."

"I just don't think he should know what we are doing. I don't trust him. If he had been a proper nephew, he'd have been at Yip's and running these errands himself."

Danny just looked at him. Andy, chagrined, said, "I'm sorry, I just don't like the guy and I let it get in the way."

Danny nodded, accepting the apology. "Yes, you need not be so obvious, nor so quick with your answers."

Andy blinked in surprise. Then he, too, nodded. It was not unlike comments Sifu had made to him, though in the context of his martial arts. Of course, he was the same person in any context. To make amends, Andy offered to take the objects to Dr. Yip's studio later that day, and Danny dropped him at the ferry terminal.

* * * *

Back home, Andy showered and resolved to attack his work pile. He downloaded the digital images of the estate sale onto his laptop. He had sketched out some material on the plane, and he broke it down now with more details about each piece, noting the medium, format, artist if known, country of origin, and date of the object. He added paragraphs that put the objects into context, such as the reasons a piece was unique and the qualities that affected the price. For the Buddhist and Taoist sculpture, he used the comparative materials in his own library. His personal library included auction and exhibition catalogs, as well as books of museum collections and his own pictures or catalogs of private collections. He had leafed through the sculpture materials last night.

Next, he added valuations. He attended the auctions in Hong Kong plus the sales at Asia Week, and had ideas from these sales. He was not prepared to put a number on the Japanese screen yet.

The other star of the collection would likely be the silver-gilded standing figure, which was about a foot-and-a-half high. He had located enough other examples to confirm that it was a Buddha of the Future, made in Thailand in the eighth century. Few came to the market. This one was legitimately purchased and it could fetch in excess of a million dollars US. Andy copied the photo image and the blurb into a separate file, which he sent to a colleague in New York. Amy Edan was an expert in South Asian sculpture, and if she authenticated it, it would bring a high price. She would likely want to see it in person and confirm that it was not recently stolen from Southeast Asia. Andy made a note to have Doug arrange a time for her to do that. Amy would likely even find a buyer, and she would owe Andy a favor if she did broker a deal for it.

It took several hours, but by 3:00 that afternoon, Andy had a complete set of descriptions and values to send Doug, save for the

Buddha, the Chinese painting, and the Muromachi screen. He put the entire set of descriptions, each with a thumbnail-sized photo to avoid confusion, in a zip file and emailed them. He included a note that he was working on the screen and had a potential buyer willing to pay immediately. He noted that he had consulted another expert about the Buddha, and he asked Doug to let Amy Edan examine it.

Satisfied with his diligence, Andy gave himself permission to turn to the Ni Zan painting. He was intrigued by the scroll, and he started to read the inscriptions more carefully. He was restless, so he decided to check the signature and seals. Sifu hadn't asked him to authenticate the painting, but it would be a good project and a nice surprise.

Andy's library included reference books that were essentially indexes of famous collectors' and painters' seals. These books were standard in any serious library on Chinese painting, and Andy owned them all. The indexes were more a pictorial reference than an informational reference. Entries included a brief biography, date and place of birth, nicknames and other names—just minimal information. The real treasures were the reproductions of the seals, a whole selection of seals associated with that name. The seals could have the name of a painter's studio, an artist's artistic name or style name, the library of a collector, nicknames, religious or secular titles, or poetic names. Under the picture of each seal was the transcription, as the seal script itself was often difficult to decipher. In some cases, an artist or collector could have a great number of names and an even greater number of seals pictured. Often, an entry included a selection of signatures from known paintings. The seals and signatures were usually scanned or photocopied from original works.

Checking the seals was one part of checking a painting's authenticity. The entries were arranged by the number of strokes in the character, first showing the seals that had one stroke, then those with two strokes, and so on. Some of the books had an index at the back, listing artistic names but not the artists by birth name. This was yet another reason why many dealers eschewed the genre entirely, because it was often a challenge to find information.

Andy printed a color copy of the painting. He started by reading the inscription: thirteen characters that introduced a short poem of four lines, followed by a signature and a date. Andy checked the date first. Chinese dating referred to the reign of an emperor, so there was no direct correlation to the Western calendar. Here, the date was the third day of the fifth month of the twenty-fifth year of the Zhizheng reign, which worked out to be 1365.

Next, he looked at the signature and the artist's seals. He checked his books for Ni Zan's seals. The seals on the painting matched those in the books, as did the signature.

Andy then examined the seals of some of the collectors. On Chinese paintings, the collectors' seals were often as important as those of the artist because they told the story of who owned the painting—a provenance. Collectors in East Asia added seals to paintings as an expression of their participation in the history of the object. In the West, ownership was more about possessing the thing, and less about an interest in the object's longevity. It would be hard to imagine the owner of a Van Gogh adding his own signature to the front of the painting.

Andy recognized some of the collectors' seals from experience. The painting was owned by the painter Shen Zhou, then by Liang Qingbiao and Gu Wenbin, all well-known collectors. There were also two other seals Andy did not recognize.

The first of the unknown seals was slightly smudged, and he could read only "Bao *something-something's* seal." Even if this was a nickname and could be found in the reference books, he would need more of the name to go any farther.

The second unknown seal translated as "Retired scholar of the Secluded Quietude Hall." Andy looked it up in all of his books, but found an entry in just one of them. The collector's name was Bao Sunyi, and he collected in the late Qing into the early Republican period, or the early part of the twentieth century. The smudged seal, then, could well belong to this collector too. Andy had not heard of this Bao Sunyi, but he might be able to find out more. He wrote all the information he had gleaned in the margins of the printout. The whole process took no more than fifteen minutes.

The Ni Zan painting appeared to be genuine, and now Andy was more than a little intrigued as to how his teacher's brother had come to acquire it. This was not the kind of painting that one forgets about in the attic.

* * * *

Andy returned to Causeway Bay in the late afternoon and walked to Dr. Yip's studio. Dr. Yip was quiet. Andy walked over to Dr. Yip's immense desk and took Sifu's belongings from the gym bag and sword bag. Yip's desk was really just a large wooden table with several chairs around it. In the middle sat variously sized boxes and jars labeled with exotic herbs like "dragons' hearts" and "tiger's breath." Dr. Yip combined these into healing teas that he prescribed to his numerous patients, adjusting the combinations until he was satisfied. Once satisfied, Yip wrote out the ingredients like a prescription and the patient took the slip of paper to the apothecary to have it filled. Today, numerous old woodblock-printed books also covered the desk. Several of the books were quite large and well thumbed, their entries showing small drawings of plants, descriptions of ailments, and the appropriate method to correct the imbalance that caused the problem.

"Dr. Yip, have you made any progress?" Andy inquired.

"Yes and no," Dr. Yip responded. He looked up from his books. "I have determined several things that it is not. This is most challenging. The substance is in the 'Dragon Well' tea."

"That's Sifu's favorite," Andy said.

"Yes. It always has been so." Dr. Yip reflected for a moment. "The toxin is tasteless and odorless and very subtle. It is most challenging. Your teacher continues to weaken. I seem only able to slow the process and can neither stop nor reverse the effects. It may be that I cannot save him."

"What can I do? Is there anything?" Andy asked.

"Chen Xiaohu asked me if you had seen the Ni Zan painting. I told him that both you and I had seen it yesterday. He is agitated about this painting—it seems to be linked to the illness, at least in his mind," said Dr. Yip.

"How could a painting be killing him?" asked Andy. "What is it about this painting?"

"What do we know about it?" asked Dr. Yip.

"It appears to be a genuine Ni Zan painting. Sifu said it came to him from his brother, some time before his brother died last year."

Yip nodded.

Andy picked up the narration, thinking out loud. "Sifu asked me to take a look at it. I think he is worried that there is damage to the painting and he feels responsible for it. It seems to be a matter of family honor for him that the painting be restored. I noticed it had nominal damage in one corner. I can bring it to a paper conservator I know in Kowloon."

"Good. That may ease his mind. Something is certainly weighing him down. It is frustrating to try to diagnose without knowing all the circumstances." Dr. Yip became thoughtful again.

Andy said, "I looked up the date and checked the inscription. I also looked up the seals on the painting. There is nothing amiss.

The seals are, by and large, from well-known collectors. Two of the seals are from a collector I don't recognize, but I think I can track him down. I thought I would authenticate the painting and trace its ownership—I think Sifu would enjoy knowing."

"It might help," agreed Dr. Yip. "You may uncover something about the painting itself that is bringing this misfortune."

"We also know that it has been in Sifu's family, at least that is what he said," Andy continued.

Yip nodded again. "Yes, but I have never heard him speak of it, and it is an extraordinary item."

"Maybe his brother bought it many years ago, so he has owned it for some time. What I really need to know, then, is where Sifu's brother acquired the painting. It most likely came from China, possibly many years ago."

Yip thought for a moment. "Both Xiaohu and his brother were born in China and studied for years there. There is a man, he is very old now, but he knew the Chen family quite well. I have met him myself but not for many years now. He may be able to tell you something."

"Where do I find this man?" Andy asked. He was pleased to be able to do something, anything that might be helpful. He was curious, too, about the early years in Sifu's life.

"He lives in Beijing now, as I recall. He was formerly a high-ranking general—he is probably the oldest and highest-ranking general alive in the People's Liberation Army. His name is Huang Malin."

Then Yip nodded briskly, as if he had just finished an internal dialogue and everyone there was in agreement. "You must go to Beijing and track him down. He will be able to help."

Andy nodded. He had been given his assignment and dismissed.

CHAPTER
9

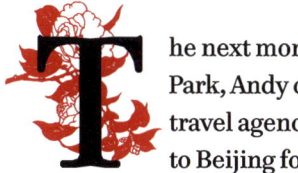he next morning, after working out alone in Victoria Park, Andy called Tonia Liu, a tour manager at a local travel agency. He asked her to book him on a flight to Beijing for that afternoon and to get him a room at the White Lotus Hotel in Beijing as well. The White Lotus was a nondescript and inexpensive tourist hotel just off the big shopping avenue Wang Fujing—a major north-south thoroughfare—and a few blocks from Changan Avenue in the heart of Beijing. Andy had stayed there before, most recently six months ago to buy paintings for an American collector at the Beijing sales. Tonia would also obtain the necessary visa for the quick trip.

Next, Andy called Itchy.

Itchy picked up immediately and Andy identified himself.

"Hey Andy," Itchy responded. "I spoke to Mr. Wong late last night. I thanked him for sending the jar around for us to see. Hey, are you sure you've never met? Because when I mentioned your name, I got the impression he knew who you were."

"It's possible, Itchy. Wong is not an unusual name. I just don't recall any collectors by that name."

"Okay. Well, I told him what you thought of the jar, that it was rare and possibly early Ming dynasty. I told him to put it up for sale at one of the auctions here in Hong Kong. He said he wanted to keep it private."

"Did he say why?" Andy inquired.

"He said it would be inconvenient."

Andy pondered for a moment. "Inconvenient" was a Chinese way of saying many things, from "you don't want to know" to "it can't be done" to "I'm not allowed to tell you."

"We could sell it to a private collector or put it up for auction ourselves," offered Andy. "For an auction, we'd probably need to trace the ownership. For a museum, we'd have to show when it came out of China, to prove it wasn't a looted object. A private collector is not as likely to have those concerns. What does he want for it?" Andy asked, at last.

"He wants a million dollars US," Itchy said.

"He'll want cash," warned Andy. For the Chinese, it was expected for big deals to be made in cash.

"Right, and he says it can't be put up for auction here in Hong Kong," replied Itchy. "Andy," he said, suddenly very serious, "what is this thing worth?"

"It's hard to say," Andy confessed. "If it is an authentic fourteenth-century copper-red pot, well, it could sell for at least five million US. It could be higher if there is competition. The glaze is extraordinary and the addition of an original lid renders it unique in the world."

Andy could tell Itchy was working it over in his mind and had probably been thinking it over all night.

"What would you think if I bought it from Mr. Wong and turned around and offered it for sale next year at the auctions in London or New York?" Itchy asked.

"Well, it would give me time to look into it. I'm concerned that there is a gap in legitimate ownership, shall we say, which could muddy all kinds of water. It would give me time to rule out Chinese ownership, too, so that China need not become interested."

"Why would China care?" asked Itchy.

"There was an auction recently where items from the old Summer Palace were up for sale—items that had been looted when the Summer Palace was sacked in 1860. Certain people in China did not like that the items were up for sale, and liked it even less that the sale was occurring in Hong Kong. The auction went forward, but nationalist issues were avoided because a wealthy Chinese businessman, who lives in Shanghai, bought the pieces with the intention that they be given back to China."

"Do you think that will be a problem?"

"I dunno, but it is one explanation for why Mr. Wong doesn't want the jar sold at auction here in Hong Kong."

"Andy, your best advice, what should I do?"

"Bottom line, I think it's the real thing. I don't know how it got here, but it rings true in every way. The quality of the piece shines through in every detail—it's almost like it hums with its own beauty. I don't know how else to describe it. The real question is whether you can come up with that much cash."

"I know. I know. It wouldn't be easy, but I think I could manage. If I could turn it around for more than five times that price, well, I might be willing to take that risk." Itchy was starting to sound excited.

"Itchy," warned Andy, "you've been in this business for a long time. There are no guarantees when it comes to art. You have my opinion on the piece, and we could take it to other experts later on. I can check some databases on stolen property. I don't think that it is, because I think I'd have heard about it, but I'll look into that."

They both knew the jar could be sold, even if it were a stolen object. A private art collector could well buy it, knowing it could never be shown publicly, simply to satisfy his or her own wants. Collectors ran the gamut, like any group of people. Some collected because they had buckets of money and nothing else to pour it on, while others collected for investment purposes. These were the hardest to please, as they were often unimaginative and wanted guarantees. Some collected for the love of it, for the beauty and joy of it. Still others acquired as a competition, as a measure of success, and still more collected from a greedy compulsion to own, to control, to hoard, and to savor privately. This kind bought stolen objects. Dealers sold to them all.

Tastes ran the gamut, too. Some collected by country of origin, amassing all things Asian or French. Some collected by time period, like Ming or medieval. Some collected by color—all white. Or by depiction—just dogs. Andy's grandmother used the expression "There's no accounting for taste," and Andy found it as good an explanation as he'd ever heard.

For sure a buyer could be found. It was important to both men that the jar not be stolen. Dealers and experts could be tainted by that kind of deal and both men valued their reputations. Andy knew there were numerous databases and other sources for lists of stolen or looted objects. A jar like this would stand out if there were any issue.

"I know. I know. But this is really big money." Andy could hear that Itchy was excited and nervous at the same time. Suddenly, Itchy laughed. "Here it is, my really big score, and it ain't even medieval."

Andy laughed too. "Yes," he agreed. "Ain't it the way."

"I'm going to risk it. I'm going forward with this deal, and I'll call Mr. Wong and set it up."

"What do you want me to do?"

"Keep working on it, try to find out where it came from and who owned it. See if you can rule out a theft."

"Okay. Let me know when the deal will be done. I'll be in China for a day or two, maybe I'll check in with you when I get back."

"Sounds good," said Itchy, and they hung up.

* * * *

That morning, Andy had received an express mail package from Cal containing a photocopy of Grandfather Brookes' memoirs of his time in China. Andy threw it in his briefcase to read on his trip.

Andy still had an hour to fill before he left for Beijing. He turned on his computer and checked his email messages. There was a note from Doug, thanking him and saying the invoice would be paid directly into Andy's bank account in Hong Kong. Doug expressed vague interest in the buyer for the screen, but he wanted to know its value first.

He also received a zip file from the Dorans—the first thirty pieces from the Brookes shoot that day. Apparently, they had agreed to shoot the Brookes' collection. He opened the file, finding about half of the bronzes. The quality was excellent—as always, Jim and Donna were thorough, taking shots of all sides of the three-dimensional objects, including the bottoms. Jim had included a thumbnail sheet for reference. Andy sent a message back to Jim and Donna confirming that he had downloaded the file.

He was pleased that the Dorans were part of the project. Jim and Donna were expert at lighting the objects properly, which was the hardest part of shooting art objects. Too much light or too little light created hot spots that obscured other details. After all, it was a sales catalogue, and the better the object looked, the more likely it was to sell. Andy added better-quality paper to his printer before he printed out the proofs.

Finally, Andy pulled up the museum store for the Museum of Arts in Boston. He ordered the exhibition catalogue of Japanese paintings sent to Kyoto that Yoshio-san had mentioned—an expensive purchase made more so by the express shipping to Hong Kong—plus an image of the screen itself. The cost would be worth it in the end.

* * * *

A few hours later, Andy cleared immigration, picked up his bag, and cleared customs without any problem. It was not his first time in Beijing or that airport. However, as soon as Andy stepped out of the secure area, he got the prickly feeling that someone was watching him.

He walked out to the curb and got a taxi. Travel in China was far easier now, though as a foreigner he always stood out. Andy rarely attracted official notice—he didn't usually travel with too many cameras or electronic gadgets, which used to be strictly regulated upon entry and exit, and he didn't do anything in public that would attract official notice.

Andy gave his hotel destination to the driver in Mandarin. He spoke with confidence, conveying to the driver that he had been this way before. Other cabs and cars pulled out after them, but none of them stood out. When the cab slowed for the toll, Andy noticed a black sedan with tinted windows that seemed to have kept pace with his cab. The sedan had ordinary Beijing license plates, so Andy knew that it was not government officials or police. "Who sent me a welcoming committee," wondered Andy.

It was China and there was nothing to be done about the sedan. Andy would have to wait for the occupants to approach him to find out more. At least government officials are obvious in their surveillance, Andy thought.

He checked into his hotel and dropped his bag in his room. It was too late to start making calls to locate General Huang. If Huang was in fact a high-ranking military man who had retired, he most likely would be living in one of the military compounds in Beijing. These compounds were all around the city. Though unmarked, they were remarkable for their tall walls and armed security gates, the kind of place that no Westerners were allowed. So Andy would not be able to inquire at the compounds directly.

Andy went down to the Western-style bar located off the lobby. Other foreigners would be there and Andy would not stand out.

The bar had only a few people in it. Andy ordered a Qingdao beer and asked the bartender in Chinese, "Does Hongxing still work here?"

The bartender shrugged. "Not here now," he said.

This wasn't a denial either, and Andy was reminded that the direct approach was not always the most effective in China. Pushing for information would not yield results. It would just brand him as the typical rude Westerner.

Andy nodded to the bartender. "Thanks," he said. "I enjoyed chatting with him in the past. I come to this hotel a few times a year."

He drank his beer quietly for a few minutes. The bartender watched him then commented politely, "You speak Chinese very well."

Andy smiled and thanked him. Andy started to chat about safe topics, the weather, the roads, where to practice taiji in the neighborhood. Americans are viewed as a friendly, talkative group almost anywhere in the world, except, of course, in Paris. After a few minutes, the bartender said, "Hongxing works here weekends. He is at the Palace Hotel during the week now."

Andy nodded. He had passed some sort of test. He offered his hand and introduced himself to the bartender.

The bartender shook his hand, a very Western custom. "I am Hongqi."

"You are brothers?" asked Andy. The bartender laughed in delight. Hongqi translated as "Red Flag" and Hongxing translated as "Red Star." The similar names, a standard practice for boys of the same generation, made it a good guess, and it would be typical for one brother to secure a good job for another brother.

Encouraged, Andy asked, "You were both born during the Cultural Revolution?"

"Nobody uses that term anymore," explained Hongqi, referring to the turbulent years from 1966 to the mid-1970s. "Now it's called the 'Period of Turmoil.' My brother told me about an American who was a taiji master and who knew about old Chinese culture."

Andy just nodded his head. Then he said, "I'm trying to find a retired general in Beijing." Again, he avoided the direct request so that Hongqi would not need to refuse a request for assistance.

Hongqi considered for a moment. "My oldest brother is a driver for an important military man. My brother brought us, his two little brothers, to Beijing from Sichuan Province. Now we do well and send money to our parents, who no longer need to rely on farming to survive. They have now retired."

"Your brother must be doing very well to be able to bring you both here," said Andy. He waited for Hongqi to continue or to offer assistance.

"His name is Hongguo, and I will ask him to help you," stated Hongqi. Andy smiled to himself. "Hongguo" translated as "Red Country."

"I am grateful for the assistance. The man's name is Huang Malin. He is retired now. I am hoping he lives here in Beijing."

"Let me call him on his cell. He may be done for the day." Hongqi walked to the quiet end of the bar.

Andy finished his beer and wondered at his good luck. He caught himself—hadn't Sifu chided him in the past? "There are no coincidences in life. One should just be open and let the opportunities present themselves." He felt a swift pang—he could not lose his teacher.

Andy watched Hongqi without staring. It was a slow night at the bar. Hongqi spoke on the cell phone for a few minutes and hung up. Hongqi served a few drinks and polished the top of the bar. In a few minutes, his mobile phone rang. He took it to the corner and jotted something down on a paper napkin from the bar.

Andy marveled that it truly was a new China. When a young person is willing to help a foreigner without fear, it really did mean a new generation in China.

Hongqi hung up and pushed the napkin across the bar to Andy. "General Huang is a major guy. He is really old. Like the oldest living general in all of China. Hongguo knows him because he lives in the same compound as his own boss. It is located in one of Beijing's old residential areas. This—" and he pointed to the napkin "—is the number at his house within the compound. You should call tomorrow morning. It is too late tonight."

Andy had been holding his breath when Hongqi started. He slowly let it out.

"Thank you," he said seriously. "If you or any of your brothers come to Hong Kong, you must call me." Andy slid his card across the bar, under a US hundred dollar bill. Implicit in the invitation was the message that Andy owed Hongqi a favor.

At 8:00 the next morning, Andy called the number that Hongqi had given him. A woman answered the phone. "Wei."

"Wei," Andy responded and continued in Chinese. "I am Chen Xiaofu's student and I am looking for man named Huang Malin."

The woman said, "This is his daughter. Please wait a minute."

Andy could hear muffled voices. The voice came back on. "Are you here in Beijing?"

"Yes," Andy replied.

"Can you find the Yanjing Hotel on West Chang'an Avenue?" she asked.

"Yes, I can find it," Andy assured her as he scribbled down the name of the hotel on a pad by the telephone.

"Please be out in front of the hotel at 1:00 p.m. A car will pick you up and bring you here. Is that understood?" asked the woman.

"Yes, yes. I understand. Thank you," said Andy, and the phone went dead.

Andy had five hours to kill until his appointment. "Where does one go to do some research?" he asked himself. Andy headed out to the library.

The National Library of China, formerly the Beijing Library, housed the Imperial Library Collection. Since the Song dynasty, it had amassed some twenty-two million books. Andy hoped to find some information about the Bao family, the name of the collector on the Ni Zan painting, in one of the late Qing dynasty local gazetteers, a kind of geographical dictionary that would list important local people and events of the period.

Once inside, he asked a librarian where he could find the books he wanted, and he was directed to the computer terminals to do a search. Andy found citations for the local gazetteers and for a book of famous people during the Qing dynasty. The latter would save him time if it included an entry for Bao Sunyi. With his notations in hand, Andy was sent to the reference room and stacks.

Andy found the book of famous people easily enough, and his luck held because it included an entry on Sun Baoyi. Andy read: "Sun Baoyi was born in the twentieth year of the Daoguang reign and died in the second year of the Xuantong reign." Andy shook his head at the last part of the entry. Technically, Puyi was the Xuantong Emperor but the title was never officially conferred because the Qing fell in 1911. Andy checked the cyclical reign dates in another dictionary from a nearby shelf. Sun Baoyi was born in 1841 and died in 1910.

He read on: "'He placed first and earned his jinshi degree in the third year of the Tongzhi reign.'" Another quick reign check: that would be 1865. All of Mr. Sun's official titles were listed next: he was appointed an imperial tutor to the heir apparent, a governor of Zhili, and, finally, he was a grand secretary to the Guangxu Emperor. Andy was impressed. Mr. Sun was a grand secretary, like a cabinet member, to the last official emperor himself.

The entry ended with three books of Mr. Sun's work, either published by him or his heirs: an anthology of collected poems, his collected writings, and a book entitled *Collecting Antiquities Studio*. Jackpot! The last one would include his holdings and would list all the books and art in his collection. Although anyone who was able to afford it could publish a collection of library holdings, it was rarely done unless the collection was important or the collector significant. Andy was eager to find this book. If Sifu's painting was indeed a Ni Zan, it would be important enough to be included in the list.

Andy returned to the computer terminal and punched in the title. His luck held—it was listed. *Collecting Antiques Studio* was published in the twenty-sixth year of the Guangxu reign. That would be 1901, when Mr. Bao was sixty years old. It was in the library's holdings with a call number.

Andy took the call number to the reference librarian. He asked her where to find this book.

"In the stacks," she said.

"Where is that?" Andy asked.

"Librarians only," she replied.

Andy filled out a request page and handed it to the librarian. She looked at it and put it in a pile to the side.

"Should I come back in an hour?" he asked hopefully.

"Tomorrow," she said firmly.

Andy gave it his best shot. "Please have pity on this poor, ignorant, and foolish foreigner."

"No! It is not possible!"

Definitely not one of the new generation.

* * * *

Andy caught a taxi outside the National Library and told the driver to go to the Yanjing Hotel on West Chang'an Avenue. It was just noon, so he went in and lunched in the Chinese style restaurant. It was peak time because the Chinese like to eat early. Andy sat at a large table, joining ten other Chinese. Dishes were already piled in the center of the table. Andy ordered several dishes for himself from the waitress. He was the subject of conversation until his fellow diners caught on that he spoke Chinese fairly well—this caused great hilarity and a bit of friendly banter. They all worked for a manufacturing plant in Wuhan and were in Beijing on a business junket. As with the others, he did not linger at the table after he was finished and he was out front again with ten minutes to spare. A few minutes later, a black Mercedes with black tinted windows and government plates pulled up. The car stopped before Andy and a middle-aged woman stepped out of the car. She was like many Chinese in that it was impossible to tell her exact age. She could have been anywhere from forty to seventy.

"Ni hao?" she said. Short for hello, or ni hao ma, which means "how are you?"

Andy replied with the slightly more honorific style used when meeting someone for the first time. "Nin hao?" he asked, and bowed slightly.

"Chen Xiaohu is your teacher?" she asked.

"Yes." Andy nodded his head.

"We spoke on the phone earlier. I am Huang Malin's daughter. My name is Huang Xianhua. Please come with me." She gestured toward the car. A neatly dressed young man held the back door open. He closed it after Andy got in and then returned to the driver's-side door. Huang Xianhua got back in the same seat she had taken for the trip to the hotel.

The driver started the car and pulled away from the curb.

"Your Chinese is very good. Where did you learn?" she asked, as they got underway.

"I studied at Harvard and I have been living in Hong Kong for quite some time," Andy responded.

"Hmm, and what do you do in Hong Kong?" she asked.

"I am an art consultant." It was Andy's standard answer.

"What kind of art?"

"Primarily Chinese art, but pretty much anything East Asian," Andy explained.

They drove a short way west on Chang'an Avenue and turned left at the military gate of a high-walled compound. There was no sign on the wall or the guardhouse, only the universal octagonal red stop sign in the center of a small guardhouse. The driver slowed and lowered his window. The guard bent slightly, glanced inside, and then waved them through.

"My father is very old and does not leave his house much. This is the only way you can get in to see him, by using his car and driver," explained Huang Xianhua. The car proceeded a hundred yards straight back, turned left at the end of the road, and pulled into the second short driveway. They had driven by about two-dozen small homes, all grey cement and each drab and entirely military. This one was equally unremarkable.

Andy followed Xianhua through the front door and small foyer. They made a left and walked through a room with bookcases and a large table covered with paper, writing brushes, and bottles of ink. Passing to the other side of the room, they entered a back room that was lit by the afternoon sun. General Huang was seated in a cushioned chair and he rose as they entered.

"Daddy, your guest is here," said Xianhua.

General Huang took a look at Andy and walked over to him. The general was a tall man and obviously still quite strongly built, especially given his years. He was bald and clean-shaven. He extended his hand to Andy. He grasped Andy's hand in his vise-like grip then pulled Andy toward him and enveloped him in a great bear hug.

Andy was at a loss. He had never met a Chinese man, let alone one of such great distinction, who was so demonstrative.

The general said, "Your teacher, Chen Xiaohu, I have known him his whole life. I knew his father and his uncle too. I have not seen him for many years. He sent a letter almost a year ago to introduce you, saying you would come one day. And here you are. He said you were like a son to him."

Andy was truly speechless. Sifu had never said anything like this to him. This affection from a total stranger touched him. This affection by proxy was almost too much.

"What is the matter?" demanded the General. "Xiaohu said you speak Chinese very well."

"Yes, thank you. I was momentarily without words. It is a great honor to meet you," Andy managed to get out.

"Sit down. Sit down. Let's have some tea. I am allowed only hot water, but you should have some tea." The general motioned for Andy to sit on the couch next to his chair, and the general sat down.

"Yes, thank you," Andy said, as he sat at the end closest to the general. Huang Xianhua stepped out of the room to prepare the tea.

"I am so pleased to meet one of Xiaohu's students. How long have you been practicing with him?" asked the General.

"A dozen years," Andy said.

"You do not look old enough for that to be the case," said the General. "I was one of his first teachers in the martial arts. He had a natural talent for it, unlike his brother, who never did care for it. His brother never wanted to practice." The General looked pensive.

They chatted for a few moments about innocuous things—changes in Beijing and the world—while Andy sipped his tea and the General his hot water. The General appeared to be marshaling his thoughts, and Andy did not hurry him.

Andy studied the General, thinking that this man was very sharp and still very strong physically as well. And if Yip thought the General was old, he must be ancient.

Eventually, Andy asked, "If you don't mind my asking, how old are you?"

The General grinned. "I was born during the last years of the Qing dynasty, 1906 by modern reckoning, in Shandong Province."

"How long did you live in Shandong? Did you have to learn German and then Japanese?" Andy asked, knowing that south of Beijing and north of Shanghai, Shandong was a coastal province and the center of the German-occupied area before World War II. After the treaty of Versailles in 1919, the Japanese controlled the formerly German area of Shandong.

"You know your history. As a youth, I learned German and then Japanese. I was trained in both Western and Chinese military history and tactics. I entered into the military when I was eighteen. I was part of the new modern China," said Huang proudly. "One that used both traditional Chinese training methods and education joined together with those of the West. That is where I met Chen Xiaohu's father and uncle. They were some years older than I was. It was hard to believe those two were brothers. Chen Dadao, who was Little Tiger's father, was trained in everything Chinese, including the martial arts. In some ways, Dadao was the essence of Chinese study and learning. He was the ideal Chinese man. He venerated his family and ancestors. He appreciated the old ways and customs. Dadao's brother, Chen Dawen, preferred the Western world. Dawen went to the United States and studied at Harvard. He adopted many Western attitudes, as well, which meant that he looked down on many of the old ways."

"But it wasn't all that unusual to study in the West then," said Andy.

"No," agreed the General. "It was a time of change in many ways. Scholars, long revered and honored in society, had no clear place in the changing China. Those in power hungered for new ways of doing things and wanted their own advisors to bring other viewpoints. Some scholars were sent to Japan to learn, but many went to England or the United States."

"The imperial system collapsed with the overthrow of the Qing dynasty in 1911," he continued. "Who knew what government was going to succeed? All we had to rely on was the personal relationships, the personal loyalties. For me, in the military, I had my commander, also from Shandong. And he—well, he was loyal to yet another regional leader."

"Yes, a warlord," Andy said.

"Yes, often called *tuchun*, after the title given to military governors of the provinces. The army was, after all, the last large organization still standing when the imperial system disintegrated. Calling them warlords perhaps better reflects what they were—power hungry young men with great ambitions and little wherewithal. Maybe too much ambition," he added, in a slightly bitter tone.

Andy waited a moment and asked, "And the Chen family?"

General Huang returned to his story. "Chen Dadao and Chen Dawen worked for the same warlord, General Feng, near Beijing. My commander also was loyal to General Feng. At one point, we went without pay for more than a year, and still we were loyal! I remember coming into Beijing at the end of 1924. I had just joined up, and we ended the reign of the puppet Emperor Xuantong. Anyway, General Feng always needed money, and he collected much from land taxes, but there were always harder times."

"Toward the end, before the Nationalists took over, even Feng needed to resort to *ping ch'ai*, which was no more than extorting money from people directly, including and especially wealthy families and businessmen. Those with merchant connections paid huge sums to support the armies, all with the understanding that they would be left alone to do their business. By the end of the 1920s, General Feng still had a huge army, one of the few in China even close to the number of Nationalist troops, but it took a huge amount of money to maintain."

"Of course, the General took money from foreign governments, like Russia, maybe even from the Nationalists. He needed hard currency, and Dawen and Dadao, along with several other soldiers, helped to find it. By 1929, the Nationalists were moving northward and gaining momentum, Manchuria was at least paying lip service to the Nationalists, and famine was hitting the General's home territories."

"Did this divide the brothers?" asked Andy.

"Not really, but their differences could no longer be reconciled after 1929."

They both were silent for a few minutes, Andy digesting all this information. He had no idea what he needed to know, or if he had been told it already.

"Sifu sent me here, in a way, to ask about a painting. Do you know it?"

"I might." Here, the General fell silent again.

Andy tried again. "It is a Ni Zan landscape depicting a pavilion and some tall trees. It was Sifu's brother's, but no one has heard of it before now. I looked up one of the seals and found it belonged to the Bao family. Do you know anything about them?"

"Yes, of course, they were a respected family in Beijing," answered the General.

"Do you know what happened to them?" Andy pursued.

"They fell on hard times, like everyone. They were caught in the transition from an old China to a new one. I remember they had a great library that had been amassed over generations. I think it is probably still here in Beijing, in the Beijing Library perhaps."

"I was just there this morning. It is now called the National Library of China," Andy said.

"Is it?" the General said, lost in thought again.

"Didn't they also have an art collection?" Andy asked.

"Hmmm, yes." The General hesitated, as if coming to a decision. "This must be why you are here. This is why your teacher knew you would come. He must trust you very much."

"Sifu directed me to the painting, specifically. But his doctor, Dr. Yip, sent me. Sifu is lying very ill, possibly poisoned. He is upset about the painting, and Dr. Yip suggested you might be able to help."

"Yip. Such a child," the General snorted. Andy had no response to this one.

"Still, he honors me that he would have you come," acknowledged the General.

"It was the Bao family collection that caused the final split in the Chen family," said Huang Malin at last. He was quiet for a moment, considering the events of more than seventy years earlier.

"The Bao family was a powerful and influential family in Beijing during the late Qing period and into the period of the New Republic. They were not Nationalists, but they certainly did not support either Russian or Japanese influence in China. They would not have opposed Feng and may well have supported him as opposed to Manchurian forces. What they were, mostly, was quietly wealthy, having kept their home and their possessions in Beijing."

"It was chaotic by 1929, with few warlords in any positions of power, and Feng was desperate to keep his army together. He sent soldiers to many merchants and families to collect whatever money he could get."

"It was more than a polite request for assistance," concluded Andy.

"Yes. Chen Dawen was expert at selling art for hard currency, usually through international connections, I think in Shanghai."

"Shanghai makes sense, since it was home to the International Settlement—there was likely many a foreign buyer or easy connections to Western sources," Andy noted.

"Yes, though there was plenty of selling happening right in Beijing, even at the Forbidden City." The General pointed in the direction of the Forbidden City, only a mile down the road, and his voice became bitter again. "China's cultural heritage was given to anyone who had hard currency. The last emperor and his brother were stealing things out of the Forbidden City and selling them as late as the 1930s, when they first moved to Tianjin, and then as the puppets for the Manchuguo under the Japanese."

Xianhua poured more tea for Andy and hot water for her father. The General took a sip then resumed telling his story.

"Dawen was very good at it. He had a network, perhaps, and some thought he went as far as taking orders from buyers, people who would ask for particular items or media. Dawen certainly knew all about the Bao collection, and he finally received permission to pay them a visit."

"And Chen Dadao objected to this?" asked Andy.

"Probably not," stated General Huang. "It was a fact of life back then. Probably always, right? 'To assist Zhou in evil-doing.'"

"Yes," agreed Andy, acknowledging the millennia-old phrase about people who actively help in the unwholesome designs and actions of another. It made him think of Sifu, who also used the expression. He waited for the General to continue.

"That house, I was there at that house with them. Dawen went out of his way to humiliate the family, which angered Dadao. The Baos were a longstanding family of scholars, part of the literati who served the Imperial Court, people whom Dadao felt should be respected, even when 'paying' taxes to a warlord. Dawen also took far more than he was supposed to take—at least that was Dadao's position."

"Is that how the Chen family obtained the Ni Zan painting?"

"Now that, I cannot say for sure. It sounds like one that I saw that day, but there were many that were rolled up and taken away. Some were taken from cabinets, too. I can say for certain that there was an argument, and that it took place by a cabinet that stored paintings. It started over the paintings, I think, though I missed the beginning, but both men had hands on a carved wooden box, one that was big enough to hold a painting. It was, in many ways, an argument that had been brewing for some time, really, one that was really an argument about the differences between the brothers."

"The rift became a geographic one, too. Within months, the Nationalists were in Beijing, and Dawen did not see a place for himself. He moved to Hong Kong, preferring his closer ties to the West. Dawen was close to another officer, a Lieutenant Wang, who was part of the schemes to sell the art, and I think they both left at that time."

The General fell silent. Andy noticed he looked greyer, tired out from the narrative, maybe from the memories. Huang Xianhua noticed too.

His daughter got up and walked over to him and said, "Okay, Daddy." She put her hand on his shoulder and he sat back in his chair, closing his eyes briefly. She turned and looked at Andy. "My father has not talked of these things for a very long time."

Andy said, "I understand. I am grateful for your and his time." Andy thought for a second and suggested, "Perhaps you would let me show some of Xiaohu's style of martial arts."

Huang Malin opened his eyes and smiled. "Yes, I would like that very much," he agreed. "Let's go out front to the street. You will have plenty of room. It is not busy—I am the only one living back here."

Xianhua preceded them, walking into the kitchen to speak briefly with the driver. Andy and General Huang moved to the front of the house. As the three made their way out to the street, the General grabbed Andy around the shoulders. By the time they reached the street, the General's driver was running back with several other young men in military uniform. When Andy looked surprised, Xianhua just grinned.

Andy moved to the middle of the street. "In honor of my teacher," he said, "and in honor of my teacher's teacher—" and here he bowed formally to the General "—I will do something from the 'Old School' Chen-style boxing."

Andy started with a flourish, demonstrating an opening that began with his hands wrapping around his body and over his head while he gradually raised his left foot. His right hand formed a fist and smashed into the left palm just as the left foot stomped back down on the ground.

The General grinned, cheering, "That is my opening!"

Andy smiled at him, pleased that he had chosen exactly the right opening to the form. Andy then began a series of movements that covered a whole range of hand and foot techniques: delicate crane, rapid tiger, and leopard, lotus, and flying kicks. These were classic martial movements, a combination of slow and deliberate motions co-mingling with swift and powerful ones. The crowd grew quickly.

Andy's movements sped up. His hands and feet moved faster and faster, his entire body a graceful blur. His audience could scarcely follow his hands—they moved too quickly, never staying in one place long enough for the eye to focus on them. Andy moved all over the pavement, to the left, to the right, forward, and backward. It was a high-energy demonstration, as Andy both expended huge energy and generated huge energy. It was exhilarating and, for Andy, it was joyous. Finally, he slowed and finished with the same flourish with which he began.

There was silence. Andy did not notice at first, but then he glanced around at dozens of soldiers who stared at him. Then a great cheer erupted from the crowd, followed by wild clapping. General Huang ran over, enveloping Andy in another tremendous bear hug that lifted him off the ground. The others gathered around and pounded him on the back.

The General's eyes were wet, and he said softly to Andy, "Thank you. I cannot tell you how much joy this brings me today." General Huang then released Andy and, turning to the crowd, demanded, "Is there anyone here who would like to show our new best friend here what we can do?"

General Huang and Andy stepped back as many of the soldiers stepped forward. The soldiers spoke quickly to one another, vying for the right to show something. Soon, an impromptu exhibition was underway. Chairs emerged from somewhere, while drinks and food were passed around.

Over the next two hours, dozens of men, young and old, demonstrated martial art forms from all parts of China. A pile of bricks and concrete chunks emerged. Piles of rubble grew, as the men broke the pieces using different techniques. Andy reveled in it—the camaraderie, the showing off, the pride of soldiers in their skills. The feats grew greater and the crowd more raucous.

Andy got up again, finding five bricks and piling them in a stack. He looked at the stack and walked around it for dramatic effect. The others quieted while they watched him circle the bricks. Finally, Andy walked over to the stack and, using a very light fist, began to tap the bricks. The crowd watched, not knowing what he was doing. Andy put his open palm on the top of the stack and a sweat broke out on his brow. He lifted his palm about six inches up and then whacked the bricks. The second brick from the bottom exploded and the three above it fell straight down onto the first brick. The crowd applauded. Andy laughed, and when everyone looked at him, he explained, "I was trying to break the bottom one."

Then the soldiers laughed uproariously, crowding around him again and patting him on the back. By common agreement, this was the finale. The crowd broke up, the chairs were whisked away, and the soldiers patted Andy and bowed to General Huang or shook the General's hand.

Walking back to the house, the General said to Andy, "They will be talking about today for a very long time. I don't think that anyone here has ever seen anyone who looks like you do anything like that."

"It was my honor and privilege to come here," Andy replied.

Huang Xianhua broke in. "Perhaps we should return Andy to his hotel, before he becomes too famous."

The General nodded. Andy could see that Huang Malin had tired.

"I have taken up too much of your time," said Andy. "Perhaps it is time for me to go."

The General nodded to his driver, who headed to the back to bring the car.

"Thank you for seeing me. I am grateful for the information about Sifu's family history," said Andy.

"I don't know that it will assist you. You must do what you can to help Chen Xiaohu. We cannot let Little Tiger continue to suffer."

The General invited Andy to return anytime. Andy bowed and thanked him formally for meeting with him.

Huang Xianhua joined Andy in the car again. When Andy protested that he did not need to take up any more of her time, she said, "It is necessary for me to be in the car, to avoid any unpleasantness."

As they reached the gates to the compound, the driver again stopped. The guards looked into the car, and Huang Xianhua nodded to them. The guards waved the car through. Andy was quickly returned to his hotel.

"Thank you for all of your help. I appreciate the time your father made for me and the information he trusted me with," said Andy.

"Oh no, you need not thank me. My father has not been this excited by anything for some time. He will be talking about it for weeks to come. And the soldiers will be, too." She smiled at Andy.

Andy was left with the sense that he had made two very powerful friends in Beijing.

* * * *

It was early evening and Andy was wide awake and restless back at his hotel. On impulse, he walked over to a cyber café a couple of blocks away, knowing he would have cheap internet access and could check his email. Maybe Peter or one of the others had left him a message.

As Andy left the hotel, he again got the sense that he was being watched. He scanned the crowd, thinking his visit to the military compound may have attracted official notice, but he saw no military types. Official surveillance was obvious and in the open. Andy headed down busy Wang Fujing Avenue, which was closed to vehicular traffic and filled with pedestrians. Young people sat on benches holding hands and older folks strolled along, taking it all in. The street was brightly lit, with fast food venders and mini shopping malls on either side of the wide street.

Andy could not see who was following him in the crowd. He walked two blocks south, turning on a side street and entering a nondescript office building. Andy took the elevator down one story to the basement level. When the elevator door opened, he heard loud music. The café doors were straight ahead, and Andy entered the bar. He passed on through the bar, walked beyond the pool tables, and entered the glassed-in room in the back. Once the glass door closed behind him, he heard nothing but the click of computer keys. Teenagers filled the room, glued to the terminals and not even bothering to look up at Andy when he came in. Many played silent video games—the volume was turned off on all the computers, or it would have been equally chaotic inside the room as it was in the bar. It was a typical cyber café, with space cut out of an existing business—in this case, a twenty-four-hour pool hall. "Another sign of a new China?" he wondered to himself.

Andy found an open computer and logged on, accessing his email account. There was no message from Peter. Andy, relieved, assumed it meant no change with Sifu. He sent a message to Peter confirming he was in Beijing and noting that his research was proceeding apace. Jim and Donna had sent the last of the images, but Andy did not download them then. He thanked them for their work and noted that he would let them know if there were any problems. Andy wrote to Cal, explaining he was in Beijing. There was plenty of time for the catalog to be finished, but Andy wanted to tell Cal that he would be taking a few extra days. Finally, he got an email confirmation that his order with the Museum of Arts in Boston had shipped.

Andy paid the attendant for the twenty minutes he was at the computer. It cost about fifty cents. Andy knew that his rate was higher than the rate charged the kids who were in there for hours at a time, but even so it was still stupid cheap. The business office in his hotel would have charged him fifty dollars for the same amount of time, and it wasn't even open at this hour.

He walked back through the pool hall and took the elevator back up to the lobby. As he walked out of the elevator, Andy knew he was in trouble—unofficial trouble. One man, slim, slipped out of the stairwell to the right as Andy moved past, and another man, bigger, was waiting farther down the hall to the left, about ten feet before the doors.

Their timing was off, or maybe Andy's was just better. Andy casually turned just as the slimmer man caught up with him. This first man was pulling a butterfly knife from his jacket pocket with his right hand, smiling as he did. Andy took a step toward the man and spun fully 360 degrees, creating momentum and a whip effect. Andy hit the man's right hand with his left, and with his open right hand he smacked the slim man in the center of the forehead. The knife hit the floor, still in its open position, just before the man did.

The heavier man was too far down the hall to get to Andy as planned. As he closed in, Andy turned and hopped back over the fallen man. The other man came on fast, determined, now that he was alone. He came at Andy with no thought as to what else Andy might be capable of—the kind of assailant who just goes berserk. The thought flitted through Andy's mind that this kind should just have a big "B," for Berserk, emblazoned on the forehead for identification. The man picked up speed as he prepared to leap over his fallen partner, reaching out both his hands to grab Andy.

Andy waited until the very last millisecond to step to the right, just far enough to avoid the oncoming assault. Andy's right hand crossed over to tap aside the man's left hand, and he struck the man in the throat with the ridge side of his left hand. The other man's feet continued to move forward another step, carried by the his forward propulsion, until he collapsed backwards on his own partner. The fallen man instinctively reached to his throat but was unable to speak. The damaged windpipe would swell and the trauma could suffocate him if he didn't get immediate help.

Andy reached back to the elevator, which had stayed on the first floor. He pulled out the red emergency button and the alarm sounded. Help would come.

Andy turned, stepped over the men and walked out the door. He continued in the busy street, back through the crowds to his hotel. The adrenalin surge had dropped substantially by the time he reached the lobby. He turned into the bar, reluctant to be alone in his room.

Hongqi put a cold beer on the bar counter.

"Thanks," said Andy.

"You look like you need it tonight. Are you enjoying Beijing?" asked Hongqi.

"I think I'm living in interesting times," conceded Andy. Hongqi laughed at the reference to the Chinese curse, "May you live in interesting times."

"I need to thank you, by the way, for the telephone number. I had great success," said Andy.

"I know, I heard about it from my brother. He missed the exhibition, but his friends told him all about it," answered Hongqi. "You are famous now."

"Too famous, I think," said Andy. "I was followed tonight and two men tried to jump me."

Hongqi grew serious. "Did they hurt you?" he asked.

"No. I know I hurt them. But I set it up for them to be discovered—they should live."

"They may live, but they may also get up again. You need a new hotel," advised Hongqi. Andy acknowledged that this was practical advice, though privately he had doubts that the man with the crushed windpipe was going anywhere soon. Hongqi wrote down the name of another, smaller hotel a few blocks away.

"My cousin is a porter there. I'll tell him you are coming and he will keep an eye on your room for you."

Andy nodded and thanked Hongqi again. He went upstairs to get his things, checked out, then found the new hotel and checked in there.

Sleep was a long time coming. Staring at the ceiling, Andy wondered about the night's attack. Who would care enough about what Andy was doing to send two thugs to bring him down? Andy understood that it had to be connected to his actions in Beijing, maybe to that day's events. No, he had been followed since he got off the plane. There were no chances, no coincidences. His actions had upset someone who cared enough to have him followed and to have him stopped. And he wasn't all that sure that he was any closer to discovering how Sifu had come to have the Ni Zan painting. He was suddenly lonely for his martial family.

CHAPTER

10

he next morning, Andy was at the National Library
when the doors opened. He went to the main desk,
where he explained that he wanted to find the book
he had requested the day before. He was directed
to the reading room.

Andy asked for the volume on the Bao family collection
again. Andy was fairly sure it was the same librarian from the day
before. She returned a few moments later with a slim volume in
her hands.

"Do you have a library card?" she demanded.

"No, I do not. I am a visiting scholar here doing research, and
I need the material in that book."

"You cannot take it without a library card," she informed
him. Oh yes, it had to be the same woman.

"I wonder if you could possibly permit me, a foolish man
who came a long way for this book, just to read it here in the library
and not take it out?" Andy asked, once again giving it his all.

"Do you have any identification?" she asked.

Andy handed over his passport. She examined it thoroughly.
"I will keep this while you look at the book," she said, and she
handed him the book.

Andy was relieved. He had no other reservoirs of charm left. The book was 125 pages long. Andy thumbed through it and saw that it was essentially catalogue entries, divided by medium, for the entire Bao family collection: painting, calligraphy, rare books, ancient bronzes, ceramics, and miscellaneous objects. Each entry was a different length, depending on the importance of the object cited. Some of the paintings included inscriptions, seals, and comments by the author. It was terrific.

Andy returned to the counter. He asked the librarian, "Would it be possible to make a photocopy of the book?"

The woman looked at Andy a moment and said, with a straight face, "Yes, it is eight yuan a page."

This was the equivalent of one dollar a page. Andy knew this was also close to one hundred times the actual cost. Why does everyone in China assume all foreigners are made of money? Andy asked himself.

Andy was willing to pay this outrageous price, as long as he could get it copied right away. Looking at the woman, Andy understood she was fishing to see if he knew this price was outrageous.

Andy replied with the same straight face, "Would it be possible to get it done right away?" He smiled as he finished.

She recognized that he was onto her and that the usual "twenty-four hours" would mean no ninety percent profit. This was her lucky day, after all, and that lovely sweater she had seen in the window with the impossible price tag could in fact be hers. She considered the request for only a split second and said, "I'll do it myself, right now."

She put out her hand to take the book from Andy. "Please wait here."

She returned ten minutes later with an envelope in her hand. She placed the envelope on the counter. As Andy opened the envelope, she made out a receipt. Andy saw that all 125 pages were there. She handed Andy his passport and the receipt. Andy had the exact amount ready and handed it over. He glanced at the receipt, which was made out for ten percent of the actual sum Andy had paid.

The librarian smiled at Andy, and Andy smiled back at her.

"Thank you," Andy said.

"Thank you. Thank you very much," she said, as Andy turned and left the room.

Andy got a cab outside the library and returned to his new hotel. As he walked into the lobby, he was surprised to find Huang Xianhua sitting in the lobby. She stood up as he entered. As before, she was dressed in simple but good quality clothes.

Andy said, "Ni hao. Ni hao. What a nice surprise."

"Ni hao."

"Did you have any trouble finding me here?" asked Andy.

Xianhua just smiled at the idea that she would be unable to locate anyone.

"My father was so excited about your visit yesterday, he wanted to give you this." She handed Andy a flat envelope. "He wrote out one of his favorite Tang dynasty poems about a great general famous for his swordplay and his student. He did several versions until he was satisfied with this one." She smiled as she added this.

"His own calligraphy?" Andy asked.

"Yes. He does not have the same strong hand he had when he was younger. But he insisted I give this to you before you left."

"I am honored that he would do this. I will treasure it always," Andy said. Andy was sincerely flattered to receive such a gift. It was both very personal and a great honor.

"He also wanted you to have this." She handed Andy a book.

Andy read the title aloud in Chinese: "*Beijing and Shanghai in the Twenties and Thirties*."

"After your conversation yesterday, my father found this book, written by a friend of his many years ago. He wants you to have it, just in case it helps with your task," Xianhua said.

"This is all wonderful. I lack the proper words to thank you. For a Western man, never mind an American, I am oddly short of words. Please convey my gratitude and the honor I feel in receiving all this. But I am embarrassed. I have nothing to give in return," Andy said.

"There is no need. No need. The memories you have provided are gift enough. The tall, round-eyed man who broke the wrong brick—that will be spoken of for years. And some of the stories he told you I did not even know. It is amazing that you were able to come here and share these memories with him. He said there were things he had not thought about in a long time. We are indebted to you," she assured him.

"Please tell your father that I will make sure that everything is made right," Andy said earnestly.

"I know that will be of great comfort to him. And you will be leaving Beijing now for a few months?" she asked, but it was really a message to him that he had become too famous for now in Beijing.

"Yes, later today."

She nodded at this. "When times are quieter for you, please come back and see us."

"I will do that," Andy agreed.

Xianhua nodded, and held out her hand. They shook, and she turned and left the lobby.

* * * *

Andy called the airline to arrange for an earlier flight back to Hong Kong. If he tried to do it himself at the airport, he could easily wait hours in line and answer numerous useless questions. He packed his bag, checked out, and took a taxi to the airport.

While waiting to board, Andy called Peter, who wasn't at his desk. He tried Tommy next, and Tommy told him that Ah Pun would meet him when he arrived in Hong Kong.

Andy settled into his plane seat. The flight would take a few hours, and Andy was restless for most of it. Toward the end, he pulled out General Huang's book on Beijing. What he read confirmed his earlier impressions of the time—the chaos, the shifting alignments of the warlords, the development of the National People's Army in the late 1920s. Merchants fared better than Andy had thought, many thriving despite the unruly politics. Other cities with international ties also thrived. Shanghai, for example, held very popular organized art sales that attracted foreign buyers.

Absorbed in the book, Andy was surprised to hear the announcement that they were approaching Hong Kong and the new Chek Lap Kok airport. Andy missed the thrill of a 747 landing at Kai Tak airport, making the hairpin turn just two hundred feet above the tarmac. Kai Tak was more convenient too, located just in Kowloon and just twenty minutes through the tunnel to the Hong Kong side. Chek Lap Kok, on Lantau Island, was twice as far from Hong Kong, despite the highway and bridges.

Ah Pun waited outside for him, leaning against the car, smoking. Ah Pun had found a convenient spot, a miracle at this busy airport. He was inventive and fearless. In some ways, Andy was surprised Ah Pun ever got busted.

They drove quickly to Dr. Yip's studio. Andy ran up the stairs, suddenly fearful. He burst in the door, startling the doctor.

"On fire?" inquired Yip calmly, righting the book he had just knocked over.

Andy felt mildly foolish.

"You can go back and see him. He is no better but he is no worse. You can talk to him if he is awake, but do not awaken him," warned Dr. Yip.

Andy went back to Sifu's room, but his teacher was not awake. Chen Xiaohu looked smaller, diminished again. Yip had placed Sifu's belongings in the room, and Sifu was dressed in one of his clean robes.

"Come back again in the morning," advised Yip. "He may be awake then."

Andy nodded and quietly left. As he got to the street, Ah Pun stepped out of a doorway, smoking a cigarette, and gestured to the car.

"How do you get parking?" demanded Andy. Ah Pun smiled. Andy gratefully accepted the offer of a ride home.

ndy slept deeply, waking at the normal time the next morning. He jogged down to Victoria Park for his workout. Peter waited for him, under the roofed pagoda. He smiled in welcome.

"Glad you're here. I'll fill you in afterwards," said Andy. Peter nodded, and the two started their forms. It was a quiet and calm workout, and the area itself was quiet at that hour. Perhaps only half a dozen had gathered for taiji or just qigong exercises.

Andy filled Peter in on the trip, the library success, the extraordinary visit with General Huang, the impromptu exhibition.

"No, no," Peter interrupted. "I want a blow by blow account of what you did. This is, after all, the only sport I really follow."

Andy went into greater detail, leading up to the stack of bricks. Peter roared with laughter at this.

"Wonderful, wonderful," he said. "The wrong one, we must tell this story to Sifu. If nothing else, this will rouse him—he will come out of this semi-consciousness just to correct your form!"

"Here's the part that's not so funny," continued Andy. "At the end of that night, I was attacked on the way out of a cyber cafe. Two thugs, one of whom had a knife. The other had nothing but anger, which leveled the field."

"Did you get hurt?" asked Peter.

"No, I was lucky enough only to do damage, not to receive it. Remember that focusing technique that Sifu helped me with at the hospital? Well, I used that in this fight, and I knocked the guy out."

"How hard?" asked Peter.

"I'm not really sure. It is still a new skill, but I think I only knocked him out, nothing worse."

"Do you think they targeted you because you were foreign and alone?"

"Maybe. At the time, I didn't even think about it. Clearly, they had set it up to sandwich me in. I just reacted to defend myself," answered Andy.

"An Andy sandwich, eh?"

"Yeah. Good idiom by the way. I guess it could have been just a tourist attack. At other times, I felt like I was being followed."

"They may have targeted you at the hotel, you know, seeing that you traveled alone, and hoped for such an opportunity to catch you," suggested Peter.

"I just feel like it was more than that," continued Andy. "I just can't figure out what or why."

Peter nodded. "Let's go meet the others," he suggested.

* * * *

They arrived at Dr. Yip's studio with bags of hot fried dough, the closest Andy had found to a donut. The smell was delicious, and Andy's stomach responded loudly.

"Can you not enter quietly?" inquired Dr. Yip.

"I don't want to surprise you and your wife," suggested Andy, smiling wickedly.

Danny and Tommy were already there, sitting at the large wooden table. They all sat down and tucked into the fried dough pieces.

"Don't you wish they put jelly in some of these?" asked Andy.

The others stared at him perplexed. Andy moved to safer subjects and gave the others a review of what he had learned.

"But I still don't know why or how Sifu ended up with the Ni Zan painting," he concluded.

"What will you do next?" asked Tommy, always the businessman.

"I'm not sure. I have to read the full notes on the Bao family collection and see if I recognize the painting. I fully expect to see it listed. I wish that Sifu had family left whom I could ask," said Andy.

"There's the big turnip," offered Danny. They laughed.

"I can't see getting anywhere with the nephew," said Andy.

"You could try being charming," offered Danny again.

"I'm not having huge success with that," said Andy.

"There isn't any other family," stated Yip quietly. All faces turned to him.

"He has some distant cousins, but no immediate family outside this room. His uncle, the one we know as Dawen, had no children. Sifu had his brother Xiaofu, who died last year, but there is no one else. He wasn't even very close to his brother, but that was more his father's fault."

"What happened?" asked Peter.

"Chen Dadao had two sons. One, the elder boy, was just like him, but the younger one was just less interesting to him. Chen Dadao and Chen Xiaohu were so much alike, so it was easy for them. The younger one, Xiaofu, wasn't like either of them, and his father didn't give him enough attention. Sometimes this is the way between fathers and sons."

They all nodded wisely in agreement, though only Danny was married and had sons. Each of them was a son, however.

"The younger boy happened to meet his uncle on a visit to Hong Kong. It amused Chen Dawen at first to court his nephew, to introduce him to his Western clubs and friends. The boy was seduced by the attention. Dadao didn't really notice, and he died without minding even if he did know. In the end, though, the connection was real enough, and Dawen in effect adopted his nephew. He sent him to England for more education and set him up in business here. Xiaofu married and had the one son, Chen Ding."

At this name, Yip shook his head. "Unlucky name," he added.

"Well, I don't have any luck with him, that's for sure," noted Andy. "I'll head out to Kowloon near the Hong Kong Museum of Art to see the paper conservator, who can look at Sifu's painting. At least I'll take care of the damage, which should ease Sifu's mind."

"Sounds good," agreed Peter. "I'll call if I hear anything from the police labs."

"I will stay here and sit with Sifu for some time," said Tommy. "Andy, would you like Ah Pun to take you over to Kowloon?"

"Thanks, but no. It's quicker to jump on the ferry," replied Andy.

* * * *

Andy boarded the Star Ferry from its pier a few blocks away in Causeway Bay and minutes later arrived on the Kowloon side of the harbor. The Hong Kong Cultural Center was right there, home now to a science museum and the Hong Kong Museum of Art, a large performing arts theatre. The Museum housed the largest single collection of art in Hong Kong, with permanent galleries and one gallery devoted to traveling exhibitions. Just as Andy glanced at the museum, he remembered they had a large red and white bowl that he could look at, just for comparison's sake.

Andy entered and went directly up the escalators to the porcelains gallery, hoping the large copper-red bowl was still on display. It was. This museum boasted a large plate, actually quite magnificent, with the red showing in many places. Achieving good glaze color in a larger piece was even harder than in smaller pieces, so the large plate on display was quite rare.

Andy studied the plate, absorbing a sense of the color and how it varied. Any doubts he had about the jar vanished as he stood there. Either all three pieces he had recently seen were authentic or they were all fakes, because the quality of the variations of the white and red were a match with the jar. He had handled the jar too, and its heaviness was a good sign. Andy would have loved to touch this one as well.

Andy was able to recognize the subtleties, the characteristics that made up the real thing. His "good eye" had made him successful. It might be difficult to articulate what was right or wrong with a piece, but Andy understood the difference. And the big jar, it was the real thing.

Andy left the museum feeling quite pleased with himself and headed down Nathan Road. Li Laofen lived and kept his conservation studio on the second floor of an old postwar walk-up. Andy had used Mr. Li's services in the past, usually to remount a damaged Chinese painting. Their relationship was a cordial one, more one of acquaintance. Outside his front window a huge neon sign flashed "shark's fin soup" in Chinese characters for the restaurant next door. Andy walked up the stairs and rang the buzzer at the front door. Mrs. Li answered. She nodded her head to Andy in recognition.

"Please wait," she instructed in English, nodding again to the cane-backed chair in the foyer.

Andy sat. If Mr. Li was in the middle of something, Andy would have to wait. Andy guessed he would be kept waiting for more than half an hour. Andy pulled out his copy of Brookes' memoirs from of his bag and settled down to read. Almost an hour later, he was just reaching the part where Anthony Latham Brookes had been posted for the first time to Hong Kong. Soft footsteps approached.

"Ni hao ma?" said Li Laofen. Andy got up and bowed slightly.

"How kind of you to visit us today," continued Li in Mandarin. Most Chinese addressed a Westerner in English, out of courtesy. But Li knew Andy spoke excellent Mandarin, Li's own native tongue.

"I am grateful that you could spare me some time in your busy day."

Li nodded his head briefly, acknowledging the compliment. He waited for Andy to continue.

"I have need of a paper conservator," said Andy. "A painting, with foxing in one section."

"Do you have the painting?" Li asked, eyeing Andy's bag.

"Yes. It's a hanging scroll. It is quite old. Is there a place I can hang it?" Andy asked.

Thus far they had been talking in the entrance foyer where Andy had been sitting. Li guessed this was not like Andy's other commissions and said, "Please follow me."

Andy did, and they stepped into what was obviously the living room. One wall had an adjustable painting hanger. Li walked over to it and said, "Perhaps here."

"Perfect," Andy said. As he removed the box from his bag, Andy let Mr. Li read the inscription on the outside of the box. Li's eyes widened.

"Yes, it is genuine." Andy said in response to the unasked question. Mr. Li did not say a word. Andy took out the scroll and slowly hung it on the wall.

As Mr. Li walked up to it, he let out a slow "Waaahh!"

"Where did you get this?" he asked.

"It belongs to my teacher," Andy replied.

CHAPTER 12

Mr. Li took several long minutes to examine the painting and the foxing in the corner. He then turned to Andy and said emphatically, "I cannot do it."

Andy let his surprise show on his face.

"It is not that I will not do it," Li continued. "I am not worthy." Mr. Li was quiet for a moment. "I mean, it is not appropriate. This is a masterpiece. You must take it to my teacher. His name is Zheng Lin and he is in the Western district. He is semi-retired but he will take this job."

Andy bowed again and thanked Mr. Li, praising him for his kindness and honesty. Mr. Li laughed and said he was honored to have had the chance to see it. He asked Andy if he would like to sit and have some tea. It would be a great favor to him if he could look at the painting for a little longer if Andy could spare the time to share a cup of tea.

Andy knew that his relationship with Mr. Li had just changed. He agreed to linger, saying, "Of course, of course. I understand. It would be like we are having tea with Ni Zan himself."

* * * *

On the ferry back, Andy used his mobile phone to call Zheng Lin, who consented to an appointment the next day at 10:00. Minutes later, Andy was back on the Hong Kong side.

Andy met Peter for lunch at a noodle shop in Central. It was crowded and noisy, but they were too busy eating to care. When they walked out, Peter told him the lab results had come in late that morning.

"It is a neurotoxin, combined with some trace element. The chemical name I gave to Yip, who recognized it. Apparently, the toxicity builds over time, and then either the dose was increased or Sifu managed to ingest something else that acted as an accelerant."

"Isn't that what Dr. Yip said it was?" asked Andy.

"Yup. I don't know why we bothered with the tests, except of course to obtain proof of a crime."

"But is it a crime?" asked Andy.

"Well, I don't think so yet. Sifu hasn't made a complaint. It could conceivably be an accident. Mostly the lab was humoring me," added Peter.

"Will I see you later at Dr. Yip's?" asked Andy. "I'm heading over there after I stop at my apartment."

"Are we supposed to meet again?" asked Peter.

"No, I just want to sit there. Just in case."

"I understand. I'll call you there later," said Peter, and he headed back to his office.

* * * *

At home, Andy downloaded the last of the digital images of the Brookes collection sent by the Dolans. He expected the last batch to be mostly paintings. He threw his photocopy of the Bao collection in his bag, along with his laptop. On a whim, he added the wooden scroll box with the Ni Zan painting inside. He and Yip might enjoy looking over the seals.

He took a cab over to Yip's apartment. Yip nodded when Andy walked in, quietly this time. Yip was studying his books again. Andy put down his bag and walked to the back, where he found Sifu sleeping again. Returning to the front room, Andy pulled up a stool at the table. He felt slightly incongruous, setting up his laptop among the trappings of traditional Chinese herbal medicine.

"Does it help to know it is a neurotoxin?" asked Andy quietly.

Master Yip looked up. "Not terribly, no. It is close enough to what I had concluded already and the treatment continues the same."

"What is the treatment?" asked Andy.

"To dispel the toxins of course. His *qi* itself is very strong, so there is no need to bolster that. Instead, we are cleansing his system, trying to purge the poison," answered Yip.

"What do you use?" asked Andy, wondering to himself if he really wanted to know.

"A variety of herbs and other curatives."

"I am going over to Sheung Wan tomorrow for a morning appointment. I found someone to look at Sifu's painting. Do you need me to pick up anything?" asked Andy. Sheung Wan still housed many neighborhood medicinal shops.

"Yes, that would be a help. I need an order of horse bezoars. I'll write it out for you," said Yip.

"What is that?" asked Andy, fascinated.

"Hard balls of fiber that collect in horse stomachs. It is helpful when drawing out a poison," said Yip.

Andy grimaced. Sometimes he was just a boy from the West.

"At least I don't need any deer penises," commented Yip, enjoying himself.

Andy ducked his head down in front of his computer screen. He worked quietly for a few hours. He finished writing up descriptions of the bronzes and ceramics in the Brookes collection. He added a section on the furniture, hoping to entice Tony Brookes and Cal to add them to the auction.

When he was done he sat up and stretched, amazed at how much time had passed. Master Yip had left the room some time before, and he returned, bearing large cups of tea with lids on top. Yip placed one in front of Andy.

"Will it taste horrible?" asked Andy, knowing that Yip prepared all sorts of tonics and would treat whatever he thought Andy needed treating for. Andy would drink it anyway, but he put up this token resistance.

"No, it is a simple restorative in a jasmine-based tea," answered Yip. Andy took a sip and found it mild tasting and the faint floral scent pleasing.

Andy reached into the bag and pulled out the wooden scroll box. "I brought this with me today," he said. "It might be helpful just to look at it again."

Yip nodded his head and Andy unrolled the scroll. This time he did not hang it up, he just unrolled it across the large table. Dr. Yip placed an elongated hardwood block on either end, over the mounting, so the painting would not roll back up. Andy noticed that the wooden blocks had poetic inscriptions carved into them and realized the blocks were specifically made for use as weights on handscroll paintings. Where Dr. Yip stored these he did not know, they simply appeared at the appropriate moment. Andy leaned over and pointed out the Bao family seals.

"I'll read through the Bao family collection tonight to find if this painting is listed. This second extra honorific seal tells me that it was particularly cherished by the owner, so I expect to find it there."

Andy pointed his finger to the discoloration in the corner. "It looks like this is damage from moisture. I had this odd thought, though. Could this be from some other substance? Could this painting have poisoned Sifu?"

Yip looked levelly at Andy. He leaned over the painting and sniffed the edges where the discoloration showed. He ran his finger along the marks, then put his tongue to his finger. Finally, he shook his head.

"There is nothing toxic here. It is a good thing that we checked it, just in case, but the toxins were coming from the tea and not this scroll," Yip declared.

* * * *

Andy returned home by cab after having a simple dinner at a local pub. He felt clean and refreshed.

He walked into his lobby and was delighted to hold the door open for the Roman beauty who arrived right behind him. This time, Andy added a classic oval face to the list of her attributes. He opened his mouth to say he knew not what to her.

"Mistah Boyd, Mistah Boyd," called out Wong Hei from behind the desk. Andy turned to the concierge and the woman walked on past to the elevators.

"You have a package, Mistah Boyd. More books for you." Wong Hei pulled a wrapped package from behind the desk and set it on top. Andy recognized the return sticker from the Museum of Art in Boston. He was pleased that the order had arrived, but he scooped it up quickly and hurried toward the elevators, trying to catch Pallas Athene.

"Mistah Boyd, you must sign for package. Everyone must sign for package," chided Wong Hei. Andy sighed, turned back, and signed the clipboard as requested. By the time he got to the elevators, she was gone. As he waited for the next elevator, he noticed he was humming "The Girl from Impanema."

He took the elevator up to his flat. Andy was surprised to find the door to his flat ajar. Did he forget to lock it this morning? Not likely. He put down his bag and the package of books, freeing both his hands and slipped off his shoes. He entered the apartment silently, in stocking feet.

No one was there. Andy would have felt foolish, save for that niggling sense that someone else had been in there recently.

Andy took out his cell phone and called Peter.

"I think my apartment was broken into," he said.

"Don't go in," warned Peter immediately.

"I'm already in," confessed Andy. "I thought maybe I had left the door open when I left this morning, so I came in."

"You are too hasty," chided Peter.

"I put my books down first," Andy said, in defense of his actions. "But I just have this sense that someone was here."

"Is anything missing?" asked Peter. Some people might have thought to use heavy art books as a weapon or shield. Not Andy, thought Peter. Andy tucks them into a safe place lest they be injured.

"No. You know I don't have much of any value, unless you are a nut for Asian art books. And I have no shortage of those."

"Anything with a more general interest?"

"No, but you know, I had Sifu's painting with me. I brought it over to Yip's studio."

"Don't drink your tea anymore," warned Peter.

"Excellent thinking," said Andy.

* * * *

Andy opened the package from Boston. He got out his color image of the Fall and Winter screen in New York. Andy compared his printout with the catalogue reproduction of a single screen of Spring and Summer. He studied the pictures. The overall composition was consistent, the brush strokes and colors were right, and the signature and seals were identical.

He checked his watch and hoped someone in Boston was an early riser. He placed a call to the Asian Art Department.

"Hello?" answered a young-sounding female voice.

"Good morning," said Andy. "My name is Anderson Boyd and I'm calling from Hong Kong. I'm looking for some information about when and how the museum obtained a Muromachi period screen. Is there someone there who can help me?"

"That's so funny," she replied. "We got a call last week from Hong Kong about some screens, but those were Japanese screens."

"These are Japanese screens," said Andy gently.

"Oh."

"Can someone help me?" he asked.

"Everyone else is in a staff meeting. But I suppose I could help. I have not had a chance to refile the folder," she offered.

"That would be terrific," encouraged Andy. She put him on hold. Americans are very good at making information available for the asking. He waited on hold for a few minutes. Of course, Americans are used to cheap telephone service, too. After about forty dollars US, she returned.

"What do you need to know?" she asked.

"When did the museum receive the screen, and was it a purchase or a donation?"

"Ummm. The Japanese screen, done by Shoei, was willed to the museum as part of a small collection of Shoei paintings. It isn't by Muromachi," she added doubtfully.

Muromachi was the period during which it was made, but Andy let it pass.

"We got it in, ummm, 1893. It came from the Landon family."

"Who were they?" asked Andy.

She perked up and said, "An old Boston family name, originally a whaling family, then shippers and merchants. I know they gave several gifts to the museum at the beginning of the twentieth century. I think they traveled in the Far East, but you'd have to get the curator if you want more than that."

Andy smiled to himself. It had been awhile since anyone called Asia the Far East. "Who are you, by the way?"

"Emma Healy. I'm an assistant here. Well, actually, I'm an intern."

"Thank you, Emma, for helping me. Does it say whether the screen had a mate?" asked Andy.

"A what? Oh, you mean part of a pair? It doesn't say," she answered.

He thanked her and broke the connection. So Yoshio had called last week. He probably had spoken with the curator, which is why he knew the museum could not afford to buy the mate.

 tchy called early the next morning. Andy was already awake, skimming the 125 pages of the Bao list. He had located the section on paintings and expected to find Sifu's painting any moment.

"Andy, did I wake you? Is this too early?" demanded Itchy.

"It's not like you cared," pointed out Andy. "You called anyhow."

"Andy, I'm gonna do it, I'm gonna buy the jar," announced Itchy.

"Yes, buy it. I'm more and more confident that it is authentic," said Andy.

"I've set it up for the day after tomorrow—can you be here around 3:00?" asked Itchy.

"You want me there?" asked Andy, surprised.

"You and the cavalry," said Itchy sincerely.

"Nervous about all that cash?" asked Andy.

"More nervous about the escort service that arrived last time with the goods," said Itchy.

"Okay. I'll be there and I'll bring reinforcements," agreed Andy, and they hung up.

Andy could ignore the day no longer, and he headed to Victoria Park for his workout.

* * * *

Zheng Lin's business was located on Queens Road West, a quick cab ride to the west from Central, beyond Mid-level. Andy had dropped off Yip's prescription request a few doors away. He rang the bell at a street level shop and was buzzed in. He found himself in another vestibule with a security camera pointed at him. He identified himself again and was buzzed through another set of doors.

The shop, which looked dark from the outside, had wonderful indoor lighting, and it smelled a bit of incense or sandlewood— Andy wasn't sure which. There were several large tables and artists' tables, many with papers clipped to them. There were sounds of footsteps overhead, and Andy suspected there was more studio space upstairs and onwards to the top floor, where the light would be best.

Andy looked around, doing a double take when he realized that one of the paintings pinned to a table was a large Lin Liang bird and flower painting. It depicted two hawks facing each other amidst a tangle of underbrush and plants. Lin Liang was an early Ming painter brought into the Imperial Painting Academy for his natural talent. He painted in ink only, using a very bold and lively style that was filled with wild energy. This was a pretty spectacular painting. Andy nodded to himself, understanding, now, the building's tight security. Zheng Lin silently entered wearing soft slippers. As Andy expected, Zheng Lin was an older man, perhaps in his mid-sixties, perhaps older. He was a slight man, a little taller than the average Chinese man, with greying hair. Andy immediately recognized the bearing and countenance of a master.

Andy remembered Mr. Li saying that his teacher spoke Mandarin. Giving the senior artist respect, Andy said, "Laoshi, nin hao ma?" as he bowed slightly.

Zheng Lin continued in Chinese: "You are well-educated for a non-Chinese." Zheng used the respectful term instead of "foreign-devil," "big-nose," or "round-eyes."

"I have been fortunate to have good teachers," Andy replied.

"Hmmm," was Zheng's response as he waited for Andy to continue.

"I have a painting that needs conservation. I hope you will undertake the project," said Andy.

"Did you bring it with you?" asked Zheng Lin.

"Yes, I have it." Andy reached into his bag and pulled out the wooden scroll box. Andy put it in Zheng Lin's outstretched hand. Zheng sucked in his breath.

"What is the matter?" asked Andy.

"I recognize the box," said Zheng.

"But I have never been here before," protested Andy.

"You are not the only person to have owned this painting," remarked Zheng.

"That is true," admitted Andy. "And I still do not own it. It belongs to my Sifu and he has asked me to look after it."

"Hmmm, I see," said Zheng. He opened the scroll box and lifted out the scroll. He moved over to the wall and selected a scroll stick and looped it through the top silk ribbon. Then he carefully hung the painting on the wall and slowly unrolled it. He ran his eyes over the entire painting.

"The damage is here," he said finally, pointing to the brown spots Andy and Dr. Yip had examined the day before. Andy nodded.

"Cleaning this should not be difficult. The discoloration does not affect any of the ink. It is a fairly simple matter. I will have to make sure the mold is not active and then I can essentially bleach out the stain. I will not know for sure, however, until I examine it more closely."

"Will you take on this project?" Andy inquired.

"I have seen it in the past," said Zheng Lin. "A previous owner came in with it a few years ago. I asked him if it had been stolen. He was angered and he left."

"Why do you think it might have been stolen?" asked Andy.

Zheng shrugged ever so slightly. "I have heard tales. I told him I was reluctant to work on a piece that may have been stolen, even a great masterpiece."

"I've heard nothing about any recent theft," said Andy.

"Perhaps the Chinese measure 'recent' events differently," said Zheng, as he turned slowly and looked at Andy.

Andy paused for a moment, realizing that once again he was being admonished for acting and speaking too hastily. Andy took a calming breath and, pausing thoughtfully, he continued. "Yes, that is true. I can tell you that my Sifu was given this painting by his brother shortly before the brother died last year. I do not know anything about it before that, though I am trying to trace it."

Zheng Lin looked surprised at this last statement.

Andy sought to reassure him. "I know that my Sifu would not be involved in anything dishonorable. But if you prefer, or—" Andy tried to say this diplomatically "—if it is not convenient for you to do this work, then I will look elsewhere."

"It seems this painting must come to me," noted Zheng Lin quietly.

Andy was not sure if Zheng thought it a good thing or a bad thing.

"I will take more time to examine it and then call you with an estimate of the time and the cost involved," stated Zheng.

Andy bowed again in acknowledgment. Zheng Lin was from Old China, the old world, and Andy thought shaking hands would be too modern. Instead, Andy bowed once more and handed Zheng his card. He left without a receipt, comfortable with Zheng Lin's reputation in the community.

* * * *

Andy picked up Master Yip's order from the apothecary shop. He was struck by the relative youth of the man who waited on him. Andy expected someone out of central casting—someone wizened, browned by the years, maybe missing teeth. This kid barely looked out of high school.

"Hey Mistah, I have some special tonic for you today. Make you hard all night long," the boy offered, hoping to land a curious tourist.

Andy shook his head. "Not today," he said in Cantonese. Surprised, the boy just handed over Yip's order, and Andy paid for it. Andy dropped it at Dr. Yip's and headed back to work.

* * * *

Back at his apartment, Andy turned his attention to the Wen Zhengming painting in the estate in New York City. It was the last thing he needed to authenticate from the estate collection. He was confident about the screen, a feeling bolstered by Yoshio's own confidence in it. But he still needed to finish with this painting.

Andy pulled up the digital image of the painting. He pulled a few books about the artist off the shelf, plus some in which Wen Zhengming's work was featured. Something bothered him, but he could not figure out what it was. Sometimes the reproductions simply didn't provide a good enough sense of the work. Maybe he was just tired.

Finally, he placed a call to Tina Po.

"Tina, it's Andy," he said.

"Andy," she responded warmly. "Do you have something for me?"

"Just my own charms this time. I was wondering if I could come by and admire your paintings tonight."

She laughed softly. Andy had worked with Tina for most of his ten years in Hong Kong. Tina ran a very successful public relations business arranging events, booking acts, providing speeches when necessary. Andy met her when she was just starting to collect Chinese art, and had guided her in her early years of collecting. Now she was known for the quality of her collection. She and Andy shared a passion for Chinese paintings—and maybe each other.

"Anything in particular?" she asked.

"The Wen Zhengming paintings," Andy replied. They were Tina's favorites and Andy was confident she would welcome the opportunity to show them off again.

"I'll make sure they are hung. You can come by for a drink, but I have a gala tonight at 8:00."

"That's terrific. I'll see you around 7:00."

* * * *

Andy picked up the catalog of the Bao family collection, returning to the section on paintings. Bao Sunyi had created this book as a declaration of love and commitment. It was written in Bao's own calligraphy, and he had added his own comments. Andy skimmed the titles, looking for something that included an autumn pavilion. He took his time, though, savoring Bao's delight in each piece. About half way though the list, he found it: the entry for the Ni Zan hanging scroll.

According to the catalog, the painting was a gift to the Bao family from one of the later Qing emperors, given to Bao's grandfather when he retired from service in the Imperial Court. The Emperor commissioned the wooden box in honor of the gift and the quality of the painting.

Andy was pleased with his detective work so far. Andy could place the painting in the Imperial Collection, then in the collection of a prominent Beijing family. In the absence of any imperial seals, Andy would not necessarily have found the imperial connection otherwise.

Andy then sighed. To find more about the painting's immediate past, he'd have to call the Little Turtle Egg. First, he called Tommy to get Chen Ding's number at his real estate business. Tommy snorted when Andy confessed his errand, but he gave Andy a number.

"Wei."

"May I speak with Chen Ding?" Andy asked.

"Your name sir?"

"Andy Boyd."

Chen Ding came on the line. "Yes," he said impatiently.

"I am trying to trace a painting that your father may have owned or seen," said Andy.

"What?" snorted Ding. "A painting? What painting?"

"I'm calling to find out if your father owned any art from the Bao family collection."

"Why would you think this?" demanded Ding.

"I'm working with a buyer and his name came up," Andy fibbed. "Did your family ever speak of the Bao family? He may have known them in Beijing."

"How did his name come up?" demanded Ding. No rapport there.

"I'm tracing a painting that may have been stolen and someone suggested that your father may have had some information about it."

"You think my father had something to do with stolen art?" Ding continued to sound irritated.

"No, no. I just thought he might have known the family or had business dealings or maybe he helped them in some way."

Andy struggled for a tactful way out. "Apparently, your father and his uncle traveled often to the mainland."

"Perhaps you think that they looted the Summer Palace too?" Ding was really mad now. "They usually went to Shanghai, not Beijing. If you want to know what they all did in Beijing, ask your Sifu." Ding hung up.

"I only wish I could," replied Andy quietly.

* * * *

Andy added a jacket to his slacks and buttoned-down short-sleeved shirt. It struck a slightly more formal note for his meeting tonight.

Like Yoshio Shubazaki, Tina had an apartment in Mid-level. But unlike Yoshio's, this building was only three stories tall. It was built a hundred years ago for British government officials to have a clear view of the harbor. The spacious proportions reminded Andy of some pre-war apartments in New York City—real entry halls, tall ceilings, generously sized rooms. The apartment boasted good natural light, though no longer any harbor views. Now the view was obscured by newer apartment towers.

Andy rang the bell and a young Filipino woman let him in. Tina preferred hanging scrolls as a format, and she displayed her collection on a rotating basis. She followed Chinese traditions of switching her paintings to reflect the season, a particular holiday, or someone's special event or visit.

Today, a day in October, the themes reflected the coming Mid-Autumn Festival. In the foyer, she had hung the first painting Andy helped her acquire. It was an especially appropriate painting for the season. As with many things Chinese, the image required an understanding of several threads of time and place. It was a painting of the poet Tao Yuanming holding a chrysanthemum flower. Tao had written a famous poem in the fourth century about plucking chrysanthemums by the eastern hedge of his garden. Since that time, he had become something like Mr. Chrysanthemum. The chrysanthemum bloomed in autumn, making the image appropriate to the season, but there was more. Traditionally, on the night of the full moon of the Mid-Autumn Festival, friends gathered together on a high point such as a hill and drank chrysanthemum wine while they gazed at the full moon. Tao Yuanming was famous not just for the poem but for drinking wine as well, and thus the allusion was compounded. Andy remembered explaining all this to Tina as they stood in front of the painting, considering the purchase. He smiled at the memory. Andy then noticed the small table, to the right of the painting, which held a more recent acquisition: a late Ming blue and white vase depicting chrysanthemums. The pairing was apt, as Tina had matched vase's date of manufacture with the era in which Du Jin made the painting—both pieces were from the sixteenth-century.

Tina entered the foyer wearing a long red dress. They kissed on both cheeks. Andy smiled his appreciation for the dress but made no comment. He and Tina were excellent friends, and she sometimes asked Andy to accompany her to artsy events, but the word "date" never passed her lips. Andy was careful to respect this boundary.

"A very nice touch," Andy acknowledged, gesturing toward the vase and grinning. "Not only matching themes but also periods of production."

"Do you like it?" Tina asked.

"Yes! Well done!"

"I had a good teacher." She smiled and looked for Andy's reaction. He remained stone-faced a moment, then smiled. "I got it in Tokyo," Tina said as she led Andy into the living room.

"I pulled out the scrolls for you, Andy. Let me get you a drink and you can tell me about this sudden interest in Wen Zhengming."

"It's no mystery," Andy said, nodding his thanks for the glass of champagne. "I'm valuing an estate in New York for settlement purposes, and the collector had a Wen Zhengming painting."

"And you want to see mine to check if it would be a nice addition to my collection?" Tina asked, half in jest.

"You'd be my first call," Andy assured her. "But leave your checkbook at home for now. I'm not sure if it is authentic. You have two genuine paintings, and I'm hoping if I stare at those I will figure out what's bothering me about this one in New York."

"Okay, let's take a look."

Andy preferred collectors like Tina—people who put the art on display, who shared it with others.

Tina had hung the two paintings side by side to facilitate close comparison. Andy put down his glass and walked over to them. He stopped only inches away from them. He ran his eyes down the inscriptions and the seals and then took a couple of steps backward, staring silently. Tina knew better than to interrupt this scrutiny.

"I think that's it," Andy said at last. He pointed to the foreground trees of the painting on the left as he began to speak a little faster. "See the sharpness and variety of the brushwork, the crispness of color application, the trees, and the rock formations? These two paintings are definitely by the same elegant hand—but that same elegance is missing in the one in New York City. The other one is well executed, and it's a fine painting, but I had some nagging doubts and these confirm them. I'm not willing to say it is genuine. Probably a seventeenth century copy of a genuine painting or something simply in the style of Wen Zhengming."

"Will it be very disappointing to the heirs?" Tina asked.

"Probably not. This group does not seem very interested in the art itself. The collection is merely the latest ammunition for the siblings' wars. And they will be amply consoled," continued Andy, "by the value of the other items."

"Anything for me?" Tina asked again.

"I don't think those objects are to your taste," Andy replied. She nodded.

"But I'm working on a catalog for a collection to go up for sale at Asia Week this spring. I think we'll find plenty for you to choose from, especially if you come to New York for it."

"I'd love it." Her eyes sparkled at the thought.

"Don't you have a party to go to?" asked Andy.

Tina glanced at her watch. "Aaii, let's go together. It's a party to celebrate my client's one hundredth anniversary in business—I should get there early. We can stop by your place and you can put on something more appropriate."

* * * *

Later, at home, Andy checked in with Tommy, who was sitting with Sifu and Dr. Yip that evening. No change, but Yip had changed the prescription again and hoped for improvement soon.

His time at Tina's party wasn't wasted. His business required a great deal of face time, meaning showing up, being visible, and meeting new people. He was wide-awake still, so he finished reading Brookes' memoirs. Brookes Senior had a flair for languages. He studied Chinese in college as a lark, intrigued by a language that conveyed sophisticated thought in pictures. He found that the ideograms danced for him, energetic and graceful. Andy agreed. Brookes wrote that he enjoyed these classes the most, that was, until he signed up for Asian Art classes. And a collector was born, noted Andy.

Brookes was recruited for the diplomatic corps—good family, old money, and exotic language skills being the requirements. He worked on issues relating to China, picking up Japanese too when it looked like Japan would have a permanent presence on the mainland.

In 1920, he accepted a posting to Hong Kong. His parents had died and he had no immediate family in the States, nor was he interested yet in a bride. His assignment was, in part, to be accessible to any representative from the many factions in China, to speak with anyone interested in contact with the West. He was a member in the right clubs and went to the right parties, and he was equally at home with the British diplomatic corps.

True to his calling, Brookes was tight-lipped about specific diplomatic activities and contacts. His love of art was fully documented, however, starting with trips to museums and dealers. Looking at objects was only a social affair at first, until he bought his first piece. He started meeting dealers in 1921, and his first purchase, of which he was justly proud, was the long hardwood table Andy had seen in Connecticut.

His purchases came more quickly after that, and he was a regular at all the dealers in Hong Kong. In early 1922, he ventured to mainland China for the first time solely to attend an auction. Andy found it curious that Brookes wrote of auctions in Shanghai, more so than Peking, now Beijing, where Andy expected sales to dominate. Andy pulled out the history General Huang had given him and found some mentions of the organized and well-attended art auctions in Shanghai. It made sense, then, that Brookes would find them. Then, Shanghai was an easier place for Brookes to conduct business, too, because it was accessible to a variety of Chinese factions. Andy wasn't sure if the art auctions were a cover for Brookes' diplomatic chores or the diplomacy a fine excuse to attend an art auction. Either way, Brookes lovingly recorded his purchases, his joy at his finds, and occasionally a snippet of history about the item.

The bulk of his collections was purchased in the late 1920s and early 1930s. He had rare occasion to add to it once he returned to the States, but not on the same scale. It was an exciting time in China to be a collector with resources and desire. The social and political shifts in China meant that foreigners with Western currencies were more welcome than ever before. Brookes took advantage of the climate of change and instability. His notations referred to auction houses or dealers, but rarely gave more provenance than that. Brookes bought because he liked the look of something. Andy surmised that he may not have asked too many searching questions.

Overall, the memoirs formed an informal catalog of the bulk of the collection, and acceptable notation for establishing provenance should the issue arise. Tomorrow, Andy would mark the memoirs to check off all the items that would be up for sale in this catalog.

he next morning, the phone rang again very early. This time it woke Andy. His first thought was not to answer it, to postpone any bad news coming at that hour.

"Wei," he said, resigned.

"What?? Is this Andy?" It was Amy Edan, calling from New York.

"Ni hao, Amy. Do you know what time it is?" asked Andy, thinking he needed different friends.

"Ni hao, Andy. It's late afternoon here, isn't it morning there? I can't ever remember if it's twelve hours or thirteen hours difference. Hey, aren't you a famously early riser? My-body-is-a-temple-and-I-have-morning-rituals kind of guy?"

"It's 4:00 in the morning here, Amy."

"Well, okay, I guess I am a bit early," Amy continued in a rush. "But I really had to talk to you. I just got back from seeing the Buddha. It's wonderful. I've only seen a few of this quality, and never in private hands."

"Okay. I get that you are excited. Couldn't you have faxed me or something?"

"Umm. Well, it was such a terrific day, and your friend Doug could not have been nicer. He was patient and didn't mind that

I handled the object. He let me babble on about it and he gave me a tour of the collection. I missed lunch altogether, he was so much fun to talk to. I'm going to write up my conclusions. In theory, I should send it to you, but I was wondering if you'd mind if I dropped it off at Doug's office?"

Andy smiled to himself, understanding at last.

"That sounds fine, Amy," he said gently. "You may be able to catch him some evening there—I think he works long hours. He doesn't have a family or anything to go home to."

Amy thanked him and hung up. Andy thought for a moment— did she actually tell me it was authentic? It certainly wasn't the purpose of the call—the call was to find out if Doug was married. Andy rolled over and went back to sleep.

Some time later, Andy awoke and looked at the clock. It was still afternoon in Boston, and the higher-ups would still be in the office. Andy placed another call to the Museum, this time to Alan Morrison.

"Office of the Curator, may I help you?" asked another cheerful American voice.

"Alan Morrison, please."

"One moment please. Who may I ask is calling?"

"Andy Boyd, from Hong Kong."

"Andy Boyd, the man with the Muromachi screen," said an assured male voice, with shades of Boston coming through. "I think we met, you know, last year in New York—some party during Asia Week."

"Sure, I remember. It's good to speak with you again," said Andy.

"Would you like to talk about that screen of yours?" Alan offered.

"I don't seem to be the first guy to have called about these screens," said Andy ruefully.

"Yes, well, collectors are fanatics, you know," commented Alan.

"I'm trying to place a value on the screen, which is now part of an estate. I was hoping you'd share with me the value that you place on your half of the pair."

"If it is indeed half of a pair," cautioned Alan. "It's not really market value, you know, but for insurance purposes we used one million dollars when we sent it to Japan last year."

"Would you place a higher or lower value on it, if it were indeed half of a set?" asked Andy. Sometimes it made an object less valuable to be part of a set, as though it were imperfect until reunited.

"In this instance—" and he paused "—I'd be tempted to put it higher. It is rare to have a complete set from Shoei, so it would be more unusual," said Alan. After another brief silence, Alan continued, "You know, we'd really like to get our people to look at your screen if it ever came to the United States."

"It is in the States," confirmed Andy. "In Manhattan."

There was another brief silence. Yoshio hadn't told Morris everything.

"Would it be possible—" began Alan.

"Sure, sure," agreed Andy. "I can make it available for you, provided you offer your opinion on authenticity in writing." Again, the world of favors, and again, Andy had offered one, albeit with a hook.

"We can do that," said Alan.

"I'll need the names of who will be there ahead of time and I can set it up." Andy wanted to limit the viewing to scholars only.

"We can do that," Alan agreed again.

"And Alan, I don't want to sound too demanding, but could you share your results with me first? Or at least a close second?" asked Andy.

Alan laughed and agreed yet again to the terms.

* * * *

Andy ran down to Victoria Park to work out. He did not want to take the hydrofoil to Lantau Island that morning. He found Peter, as expected. They agreed on what they wanted to do that morning and proceeded to work out in silence together. It was a very physical routine and both were sweating profusely when they finished.

"Peter, do you have a busy day tomorrow?"

Peter thought for a minute, "No, nothing unusual. What do you need?"

"I have a colleague involved in a large deal, all cash, and he'd like some back-up."

"Do I get to be the good cop or the bad cop?" Peter joked.

"Well, you'll be competing with Ah Pun if you want the bad cop role."

"So much for me."

They smiled at each other.

"It's the way he smokes a cigarette I think," offered Andy.

"He is an excellent choice for back-up. I understand why I am the second choice," said Peter, only half in jest.

"He'll drive us, too."

"You think of everything."

"We'll pick you up around 2:00."

* * * *

Back from his workout, Andy was just opening the door to his building when Pallas Athene walked out.

"Buon Giorno, Signorina," said Andy, holding the door for her.

"Molte Grazie," she replied with a slight accent, thanking him and walking past.

"Sei Italiano?" she asked, turning back.

"No, sono Americano," Andy replied.

She looked puzzled, then nodded and continued to walk

away. Andy was thrilled that she had even spoken to him. Then he realized that he had spoken to her in Italian because that was the language that any Roman goddess would speak. Her accent gave her away as someone who was not a native Italian, but quite naturally she had then assumed that he was Italian because he had addressed her in Italian. And then he denied that he was Italian, which was after all the truth—one should not lie to Roman gods—which must have left her with the distinct impression that he was a nutcase.

Crestfallen, he walked into his building and gave a muted greeting to the concierge. Fortunately, it was not Wong Hei, who would have enjoyed the interchange immensely.

Back home, Andy pulled up the remaining images of the Brookes collection on his computer. It was all the paintings, plus the thumbnail summary from Jim. Andy printed them out. While the printer clicked and churned, Andy gave some thought to the introduction, an overview for the catalog. Brookes was in the right place at the right time, maybe that would be the theme. Every collection was unique to the collector. Collections told stories about the collector, something about their character, what excited them, what motivated them to collect what they did. For Brookes, it was a combination of being in China at a time when great objects were available at affordable prices, having the means, and recognizing and acting upon a new passion. This would be the introduction Andy would write for the sales catalogue. All collectors recognize the passion and insatiable desire to possess things of beauty. What inspires them may differ but the obsession is universal.

Andy picked up the copies of the paintings from the printer tray and rifled through them. Astonished at what he saw, he started again from the beginning. When he was done, he had a separate pile on the side. There were four paintings in the other pile, including several details of each. All four had Bao family seals.

He pulled out the memoirs, rifling through to the marked pages for the Hong Kong years, working until he identified all the purchases—three of them from an auction in Shanghai in 1926 and the finest one from an auction several years later in Hong Kong. The latter entry was harder to find. Brookes purchased the last of the Bao family paintings in Hong Kong, some four years after the Shanghai auction. Brookes noted it was part of a small sales catalogue, just two dozen paintings—a mere handful really, all from one private collection.

There was a chance that Sifu's painting was purchased at one of these two sales. The house in Shanghai no longer existed, but the dealer in the later one—Hong Kong Arts—did. Andy checked the yellow pages and found the listing. Andy called, explained his errand briefly, and was advised to come the next day when the Director would be in. He made an appointment for 5:00 p.m. He set aside the pictures of the four Bao family paintings and went back to work on the other Brookes paintings.

He ate when he was hungry, and he sat and worked until it was finished. He responded to a sense of urgency, to the need to gather all the pieces together.

ndy woke early. He took the long way to Victoria Park, passing by Peter's apartment. Peter's mother buzzed him up and pulled him into the warm kitchen. Even at that hour, it was full and the stove was in full operation. Andy could smell that she had made a fish congee for breakfast and was now busy filling dumplings in preparation for lunch. Room was made for Andy. Andy flirted shamelessly with Peter's six-year-old niece Lily. By the time Peter walked in, Lily was busy combing Andy's hair and humming.

"You are pathetic," judged Peter.

"He just needs a wife," said Peter's mother.

"I will marry him," announced Lily.

"Okay, I think it's time to go," said Andy, pulling himself out of her clutches.

"I'll see you at dinner," Peter told his mother. "Pick up whatever looks fresh."

"Enough for Ah Pun, too," she said.

Andy and Peter looked at her, and she laughed. "And Andy, too, of course, then you boys can tell me all about it."

Peter shrugged. "Who really keeps secrets in a Chinese family? Nothing I can do about it."

Andy and Peter both laughed on the way out.

* * * *

Tommy was in Victoria Park when they got there. He had spent the night with Sifu and had come here, where he waited to work out with his martial arts brothers. He had obviously been there for a while. He had the glazed look of returning to the three-dimensional world after a meditation.

"You will be careful this afternoon?" asked Tommy, always the older brother.

"We are nothing but," protested Peter.

Tommy snorted.

"It unnerves me that Ah Pun is the responsible one," noted Tommy.

Andy feigned shock.

"You are an innocent, a scholar. You don't know these people. This isn't a legitimate sale—the whole thing stinks," said Tommy.

"Art transfers hands like this all the time," protested Andy. "And there are many reasons to sell quietly to an established dealer."

Tommy just looked at him.

"Scholars are warriors, too," muttered Andy, sulky like a true little brother.

"It's true that your apartment was broken into," said Peter, thinking out loud.

"What?! Aiyaaaah!" shouted Tommy.

Andy filled him in.

"Why do you rush in?" asked Tommy. "Try to exercise more care, *didi*," he said, using the Chinese for little brother.

Surprised by this concern from his martial arts brother, Andy nodded in agreement.

* * * *

Ah Pun was downstairs just before 2:00 and they swung by to get Peter. Ah Pun headed for the tunnel.

"Why not take the ferry?" asked Andy. "The traffic will be terrible at this time of day."

Ah Pun replied without disturbing his smoke. "Mr. Tommy said I should drive."

Andy told Peter about the link between the Bao family paintings.

"Isn't it odd to find all these Bao paintings in my lap?" said Andy.

"Not really," said Peter.

"I know, I know," conceded Andy. "There are no random acts. Someone set these events in motion, possibly a long time ago, all of which leads up to this moment."

Peter smiled. Ah Pun nodded.

"I'd sure like to know who," added Andy.

Peter smiled more broadly.

* * * *

Forty minutes later they pulled into the garage at Ocean Terminal. The attendant nodded to Ah Pun, opening the gate without giving him a ticket. Ah Pun nodded back. Ah Pun set them down in front of the entrance door.

"Friend of yours?" Peter asked Ah Pun.

"Hwl," Ah Pun grunted in answer, without really answering.

"There really isn't any parking around here," insisted Andy.

Ah Pun smiled at him and lit another cigarette.

They were twenty minutes early, and the shop was quiet.

"Itchy!" Andy called out. He walked to the back of the store. Itchy sat in his chair in front of his desk, in a nook in the back, fanning himself.

"Are you okay?" asked Andy.

Itchy glanced at him. "I'm having trouble breathing in, to tell the truth."

"All that cash?" Andy asked.

"Yah. It's over there." Itchy nodded to the table.

Andy looked at the bag on the table. "In a Bloomingdale's bag?" Andy asked.

"I'm not up on the etiquette of large cash transactions—my wife had plenty of these," Itchy answered.

Andy gestured to Peter, who wandered to the back with Ah Pun already on his heels. The parking gods really love that boy, noted Andy.

Andy completed the introductions.

"I'll stay by the door," said Ah Pun. "Is there a back entrance?"

"Yes," said Itchy.

"Go lock it up," directed Ah Pun. "We don't want surprises."

Itchy nodded and got up to make sure it was locked.

Andy and Peter moved to the massive wood table midway in the shop. Peter glanced around and shrugged, saying, "It's as good a place as any."

They pulled out chairs and sat down. Ah Pun stayed near the large front glass window, scanning in both directions.

Itchy joined Peter and Andy without really focusing on what he was doing. Sticker shock, thought Andy.

"Showtime," said Ah Pun, walking by the table. He had spotted a group of men moving purposefully toward the shop. One of them was pulling the old trunk on wheels. Ah Pun propped himself against the wall in the back. He placed an unlit cigarette between his lips.

Andy approved, both strategically—for it was a good place to keep an eye on everything—and aesthetically, because Ah Pun looked like hired muscle.

The bell over the shop door jingled and three Chinese men came in. The first was clearly in charge—the mysterious Mr. Wong perhaps? He was better dressed, and one of the others had held the door for him. Andy recognized the other two as the chatty pair from the last visit.

"Hiya," said Itchy to the familiar pair. "Came by to chew the fat again, eh?"

The others looked puzzled, including Peter. Here was an idiom that defied easy translation, thought Andy.

The third man, still standing, bowed slightly.

"Mr. Wong?" asked Itchy, as he clambered to his feet.

"It is not possible for Mr. Wong to attend today," replied the man. "I am Mr. Su and I will act as his agent." Mr. Su spoke English with a slight British accent.

"Your English is excellent," said Itchy.

"Thank you," said Mr. Su, nodding at the compliment. "But I do not know this expression about fat."

"Oh," said Itchy. "It's an American expression. Comes from farm animals. Sheep, I think."

"Cows," interjected Andy.

"Eh?" said Itchy.

"Cows," said Andy firmly. "And they chew cud."

"Eh?" asked Itchy again.

"Cud," explained Andy, in the interest of accuracy. "Partially digested grass."

"I see," said Mr. Su, seeing nothing save that Americans were gentle idiots.

"It might be hay," added Andy, warming to the topic.

Mr. Su pursed his lips. Itchy introduced Andy to Mr. Su, possibly to forestall Mr. Su's shooting them all. Mr. Su looked pointedly at Peter and Ah Pun.

"Friends," noted Andy, waving generally in their direction. Finally, something Mr. Su understood, and he nodded.

"And you know my friends," Mr. Su replied, gesturing to the goons who accompanied him. They took it as a signal, and the skinny one moved to take up a position near the front door. As before, the bigger man opened the trunk and hefted the jar to the table. He lifted the lid out of the trunk and placed it on top of the jar with a surprisingly gentle touch.

"So," said Mr. Su.

"Yes," said Itchy.

Andy stood up and leaned over the jar, examining the glaze again and running his hands quickly around it. He lifted the lid, examined the lip, and ran his finger around it. Andy then placed the lid on the table. It felt just like the piece he had handled in New York.

"Would you mind?" he asked the big man, gesturing with his hands to lift the jar.

The big man hoisted it up, tilting the bottom toward Andy. Finally, Andy nodded.

"Yes," Andy said, "this is the same jar." And he sat back down.

Ah Pun appeared behind Itchy, holding the Bloomingdale's bag. Itchy took a deep breath—breathing in at last, noted Andy—and nodded. Ah Pun set the bag before Mr. Su.

"I will take a moment and count it," declared Mr. Su, and he quietly began to count. Mr. Su obviously handled a lot of cash. He moved through each bundle of bills with amazing speed. There is a way the Chinese count money, not unlike a cashier at a casino used to handling millions of dollars in bills every day in a very matter of fact manner. Andy shrugged. Ah Pun meanwhile resumed his station by the wall, pulling out a small sharp knife and cleaning his fingernails. Peter looked at Ah Pun and at everyone else, rolled his eyes, crossed his arms, and sat back to wait.

Andy searched his mind for a topic to distract Itchy. "Hey, Itchy, how long have you been doing business in Hong Kong?"

"I dunno, maybe twenty years. I started in London first, came out here for buying trips, and really liked it."

"Was it always medieval furniture and goods?" asked Andy.

"It was always my favorite. It's what I first learned back in New York. After that, I went to London for a few years, working for a dealer who sold everything. It was there that I got a taste of other periods. He's actually why I first came to Hong Kong—he'd send me over, mostly to buy furniture. I didn't know it well, but I had a good sense of what was gonna sell."

Andy nodded at this. Good dealers have a sixth sense about objects.

"Do you do most of your buying here?" he asked Itchy.

"I do when I see something. I'd like to get to China more often. I still travel to Europe, especially Eastern Europe now. Ya just never know what you'll see." Itchy was clearly relieved to be talking.

"I find that Asian buyers, especially those in the Hong Kong area, have a taste for European and English furniture," Itchy added.

"Most of it is so big. Who has a living room big enough?" countered Andy.

"Yeah, the really big stuff takes longer to move. But some Asians are convinced that the British are a stylish bunch, so they buy it anyhow." Andy and Itchy smiled at each other, delighted by the thought that the British set the style for anything.

Andy had another thought. "Itchy, did you ever work with Hong Kong Arts?"

"I'm not sure. Do they sell furniture?" Itchy replied.

"I don't really know," Andy confessed. "I have to track down some art I think they sold, and I was wondering if you knew them—"

Suddenly, Andy stopped and turned to Mr. Su. "Pardon me?"

Mr. Su looked up in surprise. "Yes?"

Andy said, "You said something?"

"No," replied Mr. Su, aggrieved.

"My error," apologized Andy. He and Itchy fell silent.

A few minutes later, Mr. Su finished his counting. "We are done."

Itchy got up. "Let's get this in writing—a small receipt."

Mr. Su looked at him for a moment. He sighed. Itchy pulled an order pad off his desk and wrote quickly, "Chinese porcelain jar with lid," plus the dollar amount. Paid in full. He tore off the top copy and handed it to Mr. Su.

Mr. Su nodded to his companions. The bigger man snapped the trunk shut and secured it to the luggage rack.

"Hey!" said Andy, jumping to his feet. Ah Pun tensed while the skinny man started to come in from the front door.

"Hey! You can't take the case. The case is part of the deal," said Andy.

"No, I just sold the jar," said Su.

"No. No, that's not okay. For a million in cash, the case comes too," insisted Andy.

Itchy looked at Andy in surprise.

"Well, do you have another box the right size?" Andy demanded of him.

Itchy shook his head. Ah Pun started to smile.

"It's important to store art and to transport art in the right kind of container," Andy insisted.

All eyes moved to the ratty trunk then back to Andy.

"It has the right kind of padding," insisted Andy again.

Itchy looked at him, totally at a loss—was he supposed to refuse the whole deal over a beat-up trunk? Peter stood up, too.

Su had long concluded that Andy was crazy. He looked down and shrugged.

"Leave it," he said.

Su finished placing the money back in the bag and as he picked it up, silently left with his pals. Ah Pun idly followed them to the door.

Peter snorted. "What's with the knife and the nails?" he demanded of Ah Pun.

"I saw it on TV," replied his cousin.

"Gangster movies?" demanded Peter.

"Well, it wasn't martial arts," laughed Ah Pun.

"Itch, what will you do with the jar for now?" asked Andy. "You need to store it in a safe place. It may be heavy, but it is still portable."

"I have a friend in Ocean Terminal who agreed to let me use the vault. But I'll be sure to pack it in the box," Itchy said.

Andy shook his head. "No, you'll do it wrong. I'll do it."

Peter laughed and Ah Pun said nothing. They both had a fussy old aunt, and knew better than to interfere with her too.

* * * *

Ah Pun drove them back to Central, dropping them at one of the smaller side streets near Peter's apartment. He would park the car and rejoin them for dinner.

"I have to drop by Hong Kong Arts first," said Andy as he got out of the car.

"Can I come with you?" asked Peter.

"Sure, you can tag along."

They stood there for a moment, bickering about which way to go. A black Mercedes sedan with dark tinted windows quickly pulled into the small street. The two rear doors were already opening as the car screeched to a stop and a man came out of each side. Andy and Peter turned at the sound of the tires. The closest man was reaching inside his leather jacket where the butt of a gun showed. The other man quickly began moving around the back of the car. They were both moving with the speed of practice and efficiency.

Peter responded so fast Andy had trouble just trying to watch. Peter had two knives out, one with a short and thick blade, the other long and thin. With a single gesture and two flashes Peter cut the back of the hand that held the gun, causing the man to flinch with pain. Peter slashed with his other hand, cutting a foot-long slice through the man's leather coat, shirt, and undershirt without touching his skin. Before the man could look down at the opening, Peter kicked him in the chest and sent him back into the open door of the car. As the second man began to reach for his gun, Peter flipped the long-bladed knife in his hand and made a gesture to throw the knife while shaking his head slowly back and forth. Don't tempt me, he dared.

Another car whipped around the corner, with Ah Pun at the wheel. Ah Pun aimed straight for the second attacker, who leapt into the Mercedes for safety. Before the door was closed, the car sped off up the hill. Ah Pun got out and lit up a fresh cigarette.

Doors that had suddenly closed on the small block reopened, and normal activity resumed.

"How'd you know?" gasped Peter.

"They were probably following us since Ocean Terminal. Tommy said to expect trouble. I didn't think he meant an old packing trunk, so I circled back."

"Took you long enough," said Andy.

"You were doing fine. I had to turn the car around and it took a moment."

"But you missed the fight!" said Andy.

"I was ready," Ah Pun said calmly.

"Yeah," added Peter. "He had put out his smoke."

The three got back in the car. Ah Pun handed Peter a clean handkerchief. Peter wiped the knives clean and the blades disappeared. Ah Pun drove them up the hill. On Hollywood Road, he stopped in front of Hong Kong Arts and pulled halfway off the road and onto the sidewalk. There were a number of small delivery trucks and other cars that were doing exactly the same in order to park.

"I'll wait here," Ah Pun stated with a slight grin on his face.

* * * *

Hong Kong Arts, Ltd. was not much different from the many other antiques dealers along Hollywood Road. Most of them dealt in Chinese art of all kinds, from furniture to porcelain to collectibles. A big glass window made up the entire storefront, allowing passers-by a good view of the space inside. Peter held the door for Andy. The interior looked recently redecorated, with freshly bleached hardwood floors and tiny halogen lights hanging from exposed wires to highlight objects in glass cases. Near the back of the gallery, behind a stainless steel desk with a frosted glass top, an attractive young Chinese woman sat. "May I help you?" she asked, in excellent British English.

"My name is Andy Boyd," Andy declared. "I have an appointment with the Director."

"I am she." The woman smiled, waiting for Andy to process the information. It was typical for a business to have a pretty young woman to greet customers and put them at ease. It was not typical for her to be the boss. "And yes, my assistant told me you would be coming at this time." She stood up and extended her hand to Andy, saying, "My name is Tiffany Li and I have been the Director here for the last five years."

Andy shook her hand, returning the smile. "A great pleasure. And this is my associate Peter Tsui." Andy hesitated a moment before he released her hand so that she could shake Peter's hand.

"Nice to meet you," Peter said.

"And you," Tiffany said. Then she turned back to Andy. "And so, what can I do for you?"

She gestured an elegant hand toward the seating arrangement in the opposite corner, a small sofa with a chair on either end. Miss Li seated herself in one of the end chairs, and then Andy and Peter sat on the sofa, Andy at the end closest to Tiffany Li.

"I am an independent art consultant," Andy began, "and I am working on a catalogue for a private collection that is up for sale in New York. It is the estate of an American diplomat who lived in China and here in Hong Kong in the 1920s. He became enamored with Chinese art and collected widely during those years. According to his memoirs, he purchased from a number of dealers, including one known as Hong Kong Arts. Is it possible that this is the same Hong Kong Arts?"

"Yes, probably," Tiffany Li responded. "I am the fourth generation to run it. My family owns the business. My great-grandfather started it at the beginning of the twentieth century."

"Great," said Andy. "Actually, I am trying to track down a number of Chinese paintings that were sold as a group in the mid-1920s. I believe there was a small catalogue that was produced. Would you have any records? Perhaps the catalogue itself?"

Tiffany considered the request for a moment and smiled again. "My family has always kept very good records," she conceded, "and we could indeed have at least the catalogue."

"May I see it?" asked Andy, making a direct appeal in his excitement. "The paintings each have seals linking them to the same family, so it's possible they all sold in the same lot. It would be wonderful to document the time and place of the sale," Andy ended, in a rush.

"That far back, everything would be in our warehouse in Kowloon," noted Miss Li. "I'd have to go there and look."

"I'll help you," offered Andy. His enthusiasm won her over.

"Fine, I need to go there in the morning before I open. How about 8:00 a.m. tomorrow? It's off Canton Road near the piers,"

Tiffany said, as she wrote down the address on the back of her card and handed it to Andy. Andy exchanged it for his own card.

"That's fine. I'll bring photos of the paintings, too. Can I give you a ride there?" Andy asked hopefully.

"No, thank you. That's very nice," she replied, smiling slightly at Andy's offer. "I have to pick up several things from storage and bring them back here to the gallery, anyway. I'll meet you outside the warehouse."

"Okay. Well, I am glad to have met you and I'll see you in the morning," Andy said, as he stood up and extended his hand.

"The pleasure was mine," she said, shaking Andy's hand. "And nice to meet you as well," she said to Peter, as he stood.

"And you," Peter smiled in return. All three walked toward the front door. Tiffany stopped just short of the door and watched as Andy and Peter left. Outside, Andy turned and waved to Tiffany, who nodded before she turned back to the store.

As Ah Pun pulled the car out into traffic, Andy remarked casually, "I think that went very well."

Peter started to laugh. "Yes, you have a hot date with a girl in a warehouse. I'll leave you alone with her tomorrow."

Andy started to laugh, slightly abashed. "I did not think I was that obvious."

"You waved at her from the sidewalk," offered Ah Pun, shaking his head.

"I think she liked me," Andy retorted.

"I think she wants to know what you are up to," answered Peter. "Ah Pun better go with you again."

"I don't think I want protection from her," said Andy.

* * * *

Ah Pun dropped Peter and Andy in front of Peter's building, noting that he was going to park the car and be up in a few minutes. Andy started to ask, "Where are you going to park in this neighborhood?" but Ah Pun was already pulling away.

"We're here," Peter called out when they walked in the door. Andy and Peter were barely in the kitchen with Peter's mother and niece when Ah Pun rang to get buzzed in. Ah Pun entered moments later.

"What, did you run up the stairs?" Andy asked Ah Pun.

Ah Pun nodded. "It's good exercise."

"Hey where did you park?" Andy demanded. "It's uncanny how you get parking."

Ah Pun was greeting his Auntie Tsui and Lily. He considered a moment. "There is a—" and he considered the next word carefully "—family that operates maybe three quarters of the garage space locally." He shrugged. "I know them," he said, shrugging again.

Peter's mother made a rude sound. "He's talking about the Wing Luk triad and he is not connected to the family by blood. Only by former—" and here she glared at Ah Pun "—association."

"Yes, Auntie," agreed Ah Pun. Andy couldn't tell if he was being meek or noncommittal. Auntie Tsui couldn't either, but she wouldn't pursue it with Andy present.

"Let's go to the dining room," she continued. "I have already started the cooking. Peter has two very nice black bass swimming in a plastic bag in the fridge." She turned to Peter. "Take care of them while we get started."

"Yes, Mom. Did you heat the oil?" Peter responded.

"Yes, dear, of course," came the motherly response, "as soon as Ah Pun called." This, a small dig, because her son hadn't called.

"Isn't it great how he keeps in touch?" teased Peter.

Auntie Tsui made a smaller rude noise and sent them all to the dining table. They were joined by Peter's father, brother, and nephew. Cold pickled appetizers were already on the table.

While they nibbled, Peter's sister brought out hot appetizers of steamed and fried dumplings. She continued to bring out the food. Then Peter emerged with two large platters. One held a savory steamed and braised whole fish and the other a huge pile of orange and lemon flavored deep fried fish. Everyone said a collective "Ahhh!" as Peter sat down.

"So, I hear you had a very busy day today," noted Peter's mother.

"Hey, Ma. It's not me. It's Andy. The art business, or whatever Andy really does, seems a very dangerous profession," came Peter's quick response.

"And it's a good thing he has such good friends to keep him safe," she said sardonically.

"Hey, that was a nice slice through the leather jacket today. Just enough to scare him," Andy noted. "Cheap gangsters...what is this world coming to?"

"They think they are bad because they carry guns," noted Ah Pun. "No finesse."

"Thanks. I didn't mean to cut his shirt and undershirt, but that leather was thinner than the skin of a tuna," Peter said thoughtfully.

"This tells you something about who they work for, don't you think?" asked Peter's father gravely.

"They could've followed us from Ocean Terminal or waited in this neighborhood," added Ah Pun.

"It's more likely they followed Andy from Ocean Terminal—it seems our Andy is a hot commodity these days," Peter answered.

"That's enough at the table," Peter's mother decided.

Changing the subject, Peter said, "Did Andy tell you he fell in love today? Looks like my niece here might have some competition." Lily frowned, but her mother happily took up the topic.

* * * *

This time, the front door was not open when Andy approached his apartment. Inside, he checked his telephone messages. Mr. Zheng, the conservator, had left his number and asked Andy to come by his shop in the morning. Andy called him back and said he would be there.

Andy then went online to check his email. Doug had sent a short update. The group from the Museum of Arts would be down in two days. Amy Edan had stopped in to talk about the standing Buddha and potential buyers, and Doug had arranged to take her to dinner to talk more about art markets. Oh sure, thought Andy.

Andy wrote back to confirm Yoshio's willingness to put up cash immediately for the Muromachi screen and to give the Museum's ballpark figure for its mate. He also told Doug of his preliminary conclusion that the Chinese hanging scroll painted by Wen Zhengming was in fact a later copy. Instead of being a sixteenth century original, it was most likely a seventeenth century copy of an original or, even more likely, a seventeenth century painting in the style of the sixteenth century master. What that meant for the heirs was that instead of a value of 500,000 dollars US, it would be more like five percent of that number.

he next morning, Andy ran to Victoria Park for his usual workout. His qigong breathing exercises came easily, the movements flowed, and he felt calm and a sense of rightness. He began to look forward to what the day would bring.

Ah Pun was waiting outside Andy's apartment when he came down again at 7:20 a.m. "What are you doing here?" Andy asked.

"Tommy said that you were not allowed to take public transportation anywhere for a while. So I will be with you all day," Ah Pun responded.

"Do you know where we are going?" Andy asked.

"To a warehouse, Kowloon side, down by the piers off Canton Road. Peter said you had the exact address."

Andy realized that there was no arguing the point. He, too, was starting to feel that a few too many people were interested in his daily life, friends and otherwise.

A half hour later they pulled up in front of a large generic warehouse in a row of generic warehouses. There was no sign or logo, just a large black number on the building. Each warehouse could have contained any conceivable product, from plastic toys to designer clothing to electronics, produced locally or brought to Hong Kong from mainland China to be shipped out of Hong Kong harbor.

A few minutes later, a silver BMW convertible pulled up next to them. Tiffany Li was driving and there was a much older gentleman in the front passenger seat. She got out first and helped her passenger. Ah Pun said he would wait in the car. Andy got out with his briefcase.

"Jo-san, jo-san," Andy said, using the common Cantonese expression for good morning.

"Jo-san, good morning," Tiffany responded. She turned towards the older gentleman, who wore a lightweight, well-tailored suit. "Andy Boyd, this is my grandfather, George Li."

"Good morning, a pleasure to meet you," Mr. Li said, also in perfect British English.

"Good morning, sir," Andy responded more formally. "It is a pleasure to meet you, as well. Did you and your granddaughter both study in England?" Andy asked.

"Yes, we both attended Oxford," Mr. Li replied.

"A family tradition," Andy noted, smiling at Miss Li.

"It had worked out very nicely for me and so I was pleased when Tiffany decided she wanted to do the same. Shall we go inside?" Mr. Li led the way to the steel door to the right of the loading dock doors.

"Yes, of course." Andy followed.

"My granddaughter tells me you are tracking down the history of some Chinese paintings that may have been sold through our family's gallery," Mr. Li continued.

"Yes, several different paintings from what I thought were completely unrelated collections seem to be converging in some peculiar way," Andy said.

"I see," said Mr. Li neutrally, and he paused to punch in a series of numbers on the security keypad. Andy noticed that there was a closed circuit television camera above the door. The door

clicked open and they all entered a small vestibule. There was
a second steel door on the other side, and Mr. Li punched another
code into a second keypad. The small light over the keypad changed
from red to green, at which point Mr. Li unlocked the door with
a key. Tiffany went through first, then Andy, and finally Mr. Li. They
walked down a long corridor and reached a third door, identical
to the second one but neither alarmed nor locked. They entered a
large storage room, where the lights were already on. Andy noticed
additional security cameras around the space. There was a series
of offices along the wall to their right, though they lacked windows.
Tiffany walked into the first one and put her bag down on the large
table. "We can work in here," she said.

Andy set his bag down, too, then pulled out photographs
of the paintings.

"I am interested in your quest, Mr. Boyd," said Mr. Li, sitting
down. "Many beautiful things pass through our hands but we
rarely know how they fare later on."

Andy nodded.

Mr. Li continued. "My granddaughter says you would like to
discover when some paintings were sold, but it occurs to me that
you are going to extraordinary lengths simply to show provenance."

Andy pushed the photographs across the table. "I am
interested in when these paintings sold," agreed Andy.

Mr. Li looked at the pictures. "We don't spend a great deal
of time with the objects," he noted, "and I cannot say I remember
these in particular. But I do see that they share several seals in
common—surely these will tell you more than a catalogue."

"You are correct sir," Andy admitted. "I am looking for more
than provenance. I would like to pinpoint who sold these paintings
and when. They seem to be linked to another painting of which
I am a temporary custodian."

"Fine," said the older man, getting up from his chair. "I will help with this now, but young man—" and he turned to look back at Andy "—you'll need to come back later on with the whole story."

Andy hadn't been called young man for some years, and he wasn't sure he had missed it. He was sure, however, that it left him in the weaker position. He meekly agreed.

Tiffany Li had wisely kept silent during the exchange. When her grandfather and Andy stood up, she said, "Grandfather, do you need my help in file storage? You know it better than I."

"Perhaps we should all go. You need to become as familiar with it all as I am," came the reply. "I am always telling her that old things acquire dust and dirt. That is their nature. She would have me vacuum the old files if she could," he said to Andy, as they walked toward a door at the end of the row.

"It isn't efficient to keep paper files anymore," said Tiffany, in a voice made deliberately patient.

They entered a room filled with boxes and files stacked from floor to ceiling, separated by informal aisles. "Tiffany would like all of this on a database," he explained, while making a broad sweeping gesture with his hand. "I don't think it's a very practical idea."

She sighed. "It doesn't make sense to take up all this space with papers. We could make digital images and store it all in one shoebox. And it would let us do this kind of search in two minutes."

"I'm not busy," he replied mildly. She turned and left the room. The men could hear the clip of her shoes down the hall. "Now then, catalogues from the 1920s would be down the next row."

As they walked down the row, Andy saw box after box labeled by year. "There is at least one of every catalogue the company ever produced," Mr. Li said, answering Andy's unasked question.

Mr. Li rolled a stepladder with wheels on the bottom over. He slid it over to the far right and pointed up to a box with

"Catalogues: 1920–29" written in English block letters. Andy climbed up and retrieved the box. "My father had a wonderful English woman, Margaret Leeds, in the gallery back in those days. I remember meeting her when I was a boy. She was a stickler for order."

Mr. Li took the box and put it on the top step of the stepladder. He removed the lid and paused. "Do we know what year?" he inquired.

"After 1926 I think."

Mr. Li passed a bunch of catalogues to Andy.

Andy took the stack and leafed through them. Each had a printed title for the "show" in English and in Chinese, along with the date. At the bottom near the address was a stylized ideogram. "This logo on the cover, is it that of Hong Kong Arts?"

"Yes, it was the earliest logo for the company."

"A dragon?" hazarded Andy.

"Very good," approved Mr. Li.

"It was a stylized dragon based on a Han dynasty dragon that was kind of the good luck piece in my grandfather's collection. The dragon sits in my living room today."

"I think I've seen this before," noted Andy. "Do you still use it on catalogues or cards?"

"Not anymore." Mr. Li shook his head in regret. "The new management thinks it looks old fashioned."

"New is not always better," argued Andy. He opened the first catalogue from 1927.

It was very simply produced, written in English with a minimum of information and numerous strange spellings of Chinese words.

It was slow going, as Andy considered the phonetic and literal entries. In the third catalogue, Andy found what he was looking for—a listing that showed when the Bao family paintings were sold to Brookes. And in the same lot, a listing for a Ni Zan—spelled Nee Tson—landscape painting entitled "Autumn Pavilion." Andy's pulse quickened. Here was Sifu's painting—well, Sifu's brother's painting—listed for sale in 1929. It was an important piece of information.

"Do you have a record of who bought these paintings?" Andy asked excitedly, barely able to contain himself.

"That is more complicated. But now that we have a confirmed date, we can track the files from 1929," Mr. Li said, and he headed down another aisle. "Let's see what Miss Leeds left us with."

"These paintings all came from a private collection owned by a prominent Beijing family named Bao. I think they were used as collateral and hard currency for a warlord in northern China in the 1920s. I am sure you will find that these were purchased by an Anthony Brookes," said Andy, pointing to the entries. "It is for his estate that I am writing a catalogue, for a sale in New York. He was a diplomat and purchased Chinese art here in Hong Kong and also in Beijing and Shanghai during the mid-to-late 1920s and 30s."

Mr. Li nodded and ran his finger down a row of boxes.

"But I think this painting, entry number seventeen, is the more interesting find in the catalogue," Andy continued. "It has recently come into my possession for safe keeping and I am trying to find out about its history."

Mr. Li pointed to another box, this one marked "Receivables 1929." Andy pulled it out and carried it to a small table.

Inside were yellowed papers, tied in bundles. Mr. Li set aside the first few and then smiled. "Well, bless Miss Leeds. Here are the receipts from that very sale." He untied the bundle and turned over the pages one by one. "According to the file, all of the paintings except for six were sold. Mr. Brookes seems to have purchased four of them. He had a hold on a fifth painting but did not buy it. The 'Nee Tson' was not sold but returned to the agent with the other unsold paintings."

"Does it list the agent?" Andy asked.

"Oh, yes. A Chen Dawen and a Wang Shenming are listed as the agents on these sales receipts." Mr. Li turned the paper so Andy could see.

"It seems a little strange, but Mr. Chen apparently bought the remaining paintings himself, or at least he kept them for future sale," Mr. Li stated. "The paintings originally came in from Shanghai. Hong Kong Arts took care of the shipping. These notes say that the items were returned to Shanghai to Chen or his partner, but this handwritten note indicates otherwise."

Andy leaned over again and saw the faded ink notation: "Items returned to M. Chen, Hong Kong address. M. Leeds."

"Maybe there was a period when shipping to Shanghai wasn't very safe," offered Andy.

"Oh, I don't think so," said Mr. Li. "Back then, we did a huge business in shipping alone. We sent art all over the world, and we acted as shipping agents for a great deal of art leaving China. It was a bit before my time, but I don't think we ever ran into trouble."

The two heard the hurried clip-clip of shoes in the hall. Tiffany Li returned.

"Grandfather, are we ready to go? I need to open the gallery at 11:00." She looked pointedly at her watch. Impatient, she was less attractive to Andy.

"My dear, let us make some copies of these pages for our friend," Mr. Li said, handing her the receipts.

They watched her depart. Clip, clip, clip. Mr. Li sighed. "She is very good at the business," he commented. "Now, you may keep that copy of the catalogue. It is an extra, and I'll be glad to know that some paper copies will exist after Tiffany is done."

Andy knew he, too, had to leave to make his next appointment, but he was reluctant to go. He spent so much time in the past, and knew that this room with its remnants held dozens more secrets. He thought Mr. Li had enjoyed finding these answers.

Tiffany Li returned, clip, clip, clip, with his copies. Andy added them to the other pages in his bag.

"Was that all you needed?" she asked politely.

"Yes, I was looking for the dates of sale for the paintings and I learned some other details, too. I have the name of the agent and I may even be able to trace him."

"Not everyone wants their sales scrutinized, Mr. Boyd. This business has always been legitimate and we would have made sure the agent had authority to sell the paintings. Otherwise, I would not have allowed this meeting. But it was a dangerous time for many who might not want their stories told."

"Stories have a way of coming out," Andy protested.

"Only if you let them," she said, as she let him out the exit doors.

* * * *

Andy was quiet while Ah Pun drove back to Hong Kong and Mr. Zheng's studio.

Tommy rang on his mobile phone just before Andy reached the conservator's door.

"Sifu is great. Dr. Yip expects him to be awake and lucid by lunchtime."

"Excellent."

"Yes. I'll meet you there as soon as I can. Hey, how'd it go with the girl?"

"She doesn't seem very interested in the past," said Andy sadly, acknowledging out loud the seriousness of the defect.

"Maybe you need to find a girl from the past," suggested Tommy.

* * * *

Mr. Zheng buzzed Andy through both sets of doors into the studio. Andy instantly remembered the smell of sandlewood incense. Mr. Zheng waited for him by a table on which he had placed the box that held the Ni Zan painting. Andy bowed slightly to show respect. Mr. Zheng returned a slight, graceful bow. Andy walked to the side of the table opposite Mr. Zheng and waited for him to speak.

"Thank you for coming."

"I am pleased to return," Andy said.

"When you were last here, I mentioned that this painting—" Mr. Zheng lifted his hand and opened his fingers in the direction of the box "—'must come to me' is, I believe, what I said."

"Yes, apparently I wasn't the first to bring it in," Andy agreed.

"Yes, it was shown to me several years ago. A young man, not much older than yourself, brought it here." Mr. Zheng closed his eyes to recollect. "He asked if the damage should be repaired, whether that would affect the value of the painting, what I thought it was worth, and so on." Again he opened his fingers in his hand gesture.

"Do you remember his name?" Andy interrupted.

Mr. Zheng continued, "We never got that far. I told him that the painting was stolen. He became extremely angry and without saying another word left with the painting. I have not seen the painting since."

"I see," Andy said, taking a moment. Andy guessed that Mr. Zheng had been thinking hard about something and could not be rushed. "How is it that you knew the painting was stolen?" Andy asked.

"Yes, yes. Your question gets to the heart of the matter," Mr. Zheng answered. "I have debated whether to discuss this matter at all with you. But it seems that the time has come. The painting used to belong to my family."

Andy hadn't seen that coming—Sifu, with stolen art? Andy started to frown. "The painting was part of my grandfather's collection, my mother's father," explained Mr. Zheng. "My family had lived in Beijing for many generations."

"Did they know the Bao family?" interjected Andy, finding his tongue again.

"Yes," he answered sadly. "They knew that old family. But the Bao family exists no more."

"I'm sorry they are all dead," said Andy quietly.

"The turn of the last century was hard on them. They had been scholar officials for generations, always loyal to the emperor. When the Manchu government fell in 1911, the Baos found themselves unable to change. So many governments came and went, some not even Chinese."

"Was Bao Sunyi your maternal grandfather?" Andy asked quietly.

"Yes. How is it that you know this?"

Andy placed his briefcase on the table and removed the photocopy of *Collecting Antiquities Studio*, the book of the Bao family collection. "I got this in Beijing recently, at the National Library of China."

Andy handed the photocopied book to Mr. Zheng. Mr. Zheng blew out air softly and stroked the cover.

"I have been trying to piece together all these seemingly separate pieces to a puzzle I still do not yet understand, and you are part of this puzzle," Andy continued. "I have been recently tracking down a number of paintings that were in your family's collection, including, it appears, this painting." Andy pointed toward the box on the table.

"I am indeed pleased that I have asked you here today," Mr. Zheng added. "We both realize that this meeting is not a matter of chance. I am pleased to see that you have read this," said Mr.

Zheng, holding up the clipped pages. "I have my own copy, of course." Mr. Zheng turned and picked up a small pile of books and documents. On the top was a small book much like the one Andy had seen in Beijing.

"You could have saved me a trip to Beijing. But then, we both had to get here today along our own paths," Andy remarked thoughtfully.

"Well said, young man," noted Mr. Zheng. "Now, I think you can be of assistance to me."

"Yes?" Andy asked.

"Have you read the entire book?" Mr. Zheng asked.

"Not yet. I was focusing on this painting and four others from a private collection in the US," Andy answered sheepishly.

"What you haven't found yet, I'm sure, is this list," said Mr. Zheng. He pulled a folio from the stack of books and opened it to the two sheets of paper mounted inside. "This is the list of objects taken from my family by warlords. You will notice that there is a mark next to some of the objects—those are the objects I have found. I am attempting to locate the objects that have no mark next to them. My mother asked me to do this, to keep this record and record where each piece has gone. Here—" and Mr. Zheng opened a small notebook "—is recorded where these objects can be found today."

Mr. Zheng looked intently at Andy. After a moment, Mr. Zheng said, "I am not, I mean, my family is not interested in getting these back. We need to know where they are, that they are cared for properly. It is more a matter of pride and a kind of closure. This may seem strange to you. You are probably thinking that these things belonged to my family and there must be reparations for the loss. But you know we Chinese view history in a nonlinear way, a way very different than in the West. We were able to participate in the history of these things. There is no real need for a single person or a single family to own these things—no sense that the art is ours, to do with what we want. This is great art. Our responsibility is to ensure its safekeeping. These things are part of our cultural heritage, a very old heritage. They belong to all of China, to all the world. No single person should decide the fate of these things. Our family understood that they were merely safe-keeping these things until the time came for them to go to the next caretaker."

Andy looked thoughtfully at Mr. Zheng. He was unusually quiet as he pondered the meanings of these statements. Mr. Zheng continued, "I am also getting old and need neither the money nor the responsibility."

Andy took the folio and examined the list. "This is quite extraordinary. I do indeed know the location of these four paintings." Andy pointed to the Brookes paintings. "And I see here that this Ni Zan painting is also on the list." Andy pointed again to the box on the table. "Most of the rest of these paintings were in a sales catalogue from 1929. I do not know their location today. But the sale was at Hong Kong Arts and I was at their warehouse this morning. I can give you a copy of the sales catalogue, and we may be able to find out more." Andy looked up at Mr. Zheng.

Andy looked at the rest of the list and had another moment of disconnect when his eyes registered something and his brain struggled to keep up. "It says here: a large Yuan dynasty jar, with lid, white with red glaze."

"Oh, yes. It is listed in the Bao Family collection book that you have." Mr. Zheng said. He took up his copy and began to search quickly through it. "Here it is recorded—" he showed Andy the page "—with a special note that the lid is original to the piece and not a later replacement, making this jar and lid combination very rare."

Andy started to get the funny feeling back.

"Was it a tea jar?" he asked, gesturing with his hands as if the jar and lid were six or eight inches high.

"Oh no," laughed Mr. Zheng. "It was a full-sized jar." He spread Andy's hands about two feet apart. "It was one of my grandfather's cherished possessions—the family had gone to great lengths at different times to protect it. In times of war, it would be hidden away, and the day the soldiers came, my grandfather was packing it up. He guessed wrong about the kind of trouble the family was in, so the solders found it too. My mother said he could not bear the shame, that after generations of safe keeping he had failed to keep it safe."

Andy shook his head slowly in amazement. "I've seen a large red and white jar lately," he confessed, "though I can't say that it came from a warlord's collection."

"It's not likely to have stayed in any General's collection," noted Mr. Zheng. "It would have been far too valuable to hold on to—those men needed money."

"How did it get confiscated?" asked Andy.

"My mother told me—and remember that she was barely in her teens at this time—that her father had become scared, truly scared, by events in Beijing. He had tried to act like it was nothing, that it would pass soon enough, but he finally realized the danger.

"For years, when the Bao family sensed danger, the jar was packed up with other special possessions and moved to safety. The morning the soldiers came, my mother remembers standing in the living room—she and her father had already packed away smaller items, jewels, valuable jades, delicate lacquer boxes, silks. They heard the soldiers coming and my mother was sent away to hide. She heard shouting, the servants crying, doors slamming. When it was over, she found her father still in the living room, looking like a broken man. He made my mother follow him through the house, making a list of all the things taken. The soldiers had taken several loads, mostly paintings. They didn't find the items packed away, but they took whatever was portable."

"A huge porcelain jar was portable?" asked Andy in disbelief.

Mr. Zheng laughed at this.

"Amazing, isn't it? But it was easy to move—it had already been packed for transport."

Zheng handed Andy another set of the folio pages. "Anyway, this is my mother's list—the last amendment to the collection book."

Andy stared at the folio pages for a moment, thinking furiously. Itchy's jar from a warlord's forced sale? It could explain why no record of the jar existed, why dealers hadn't heard of one, and how it had stayed out of sight for so long.

"I think I might know where your jar is," he said slowly.

"It's not my jar," corrected Mr. Zheng gently. "We have only been custodians. In the following years, my mother traced what she could. It was a personal mission of hers, to make sure the pieces were safe."

"That they had good homes," offered Andy, and Zheng nodded.

"She would identify the pieces, then try to give the owners the provenance, try to make them appreciate the task of safeguarding. It had to do with honor."

"So her father would not have failed," concluded Andy.

"Just so."

"Then this Ni Zan painting really belongs with your family. I understand why you are hesitant to work on it. I had no idea why you would be reluctant, unless it was an ill omen or something. What a muddle."

"Why don't you leave the painting here for now and let me restore it properly. I would be glad of it. Maybe it is a new form of closure."

Andy agreed to leave the painting for repair. "I will try to help you with your list," he added, "and I'm hopeful that my Sifu can help sort it out."

"You are an unusual messenger, at least by Chinese allegorical standards," mused Mr. Zheng. "Yes, well, a dragon or a lion would be too obvious, even in Hong Kong."

This time the two men shook hands as they parted.

Andy's mind raced as Ah Pun sped to Dr. Yip's apartment and Sifu. Andy felt it a marvelous twist to find a Bao descendant repairing the painting and the family honor at the same time. Life rarely offered such elegant connections and conclusions.

* * * *

Andy burst into Dr. Yip's studio and stumbled to a halt when five pairs of eyes turned his way. Dr. Yip, Tommy, Danny, Peter, and, most importantly, Sifu were grouped in the living room. They had been talking quietly. Andy suddenly felt clumsy and his own breath sounded loud in his ears.

"It's about time," Danny said as he put his finger to his lips, signaling Andy to settle down. "Did Ah Pun actually obey speed limits?"

But Andy's attention was focused on Sifu, and he examined his teacher's face for signs of vitality. Sifu did look well, with good color in his face and assurance in his movements. Sifu smiled gently at Andy's examination. Andy nodded, content with what he saw.

"Andy, why don't you come get a cup of tea," offered Dr. Yip, who stood and moved to the kitchen. Andy trailed behind, reluctant to leave Sifu's side.

"He's fine, Andy" reassured Dr. Yip. "Improving very quickly, which is no surprise considering the strength of his *qi*."

Dr. Yip looked at Andy, considered a moment, and selected a decoction in a glass jar. He poured some of the concentrated liquid into a small enamel pot and set it to heat on the stove.

He added some hot water and poured it into a tall cup, onto which he fitted a lid.

The warm vessel felt good in Andy's hands, and he lifted the lid and took a sip. He could feel the calm slip over him, and he closed his eyes briefly to savor it. When he opened them again, Dr. Yip was grinning, clearly delighted with himself.

"Yes, yes, just so," he agreed with Andy's pleasure. "I made that tonic up just for you. I will write the prescription and you will get it filled at the same shop. Usually, you should take it before meals."

Andy opened his mouth to protest, but then he shrugged his agreement. It really was good.

"Of course it's good," said Dr. Yip, reading Andy's mind. "For my young American friend I added extra flavors."

"This native New Yorker thanks you," Andy said with a small bow.

Dr. Yip gestured for Andy to precede him out of the kitchen, and they both returned to the living room. Yip returned to his place on the larger couch next to Sifu. The others had taken chairs around Dr. Yip's Mahjong table. Andy sat on the small couch to the side. The others paused again and they all looked at Andy, who they knew would have to speak. "Sifu, I am so happy to see you up and about."

"I am not much on the 'about,' but I too am pleased." Sifu bowed slightly to the elder Dr. Yip.

"I was there when you were born, and I won't suffer to let you precede me into the next life," Dr. Yip responded. "And, it was not your time."

"Indeed," replied Sifu, who reflected on his own thoughts for a moment. "Well, Andy, it seems you have kept busy without me. There are many streams that are joining together for you, have you reconciled them yet?"

"No, but I think I've fallen into all of them. I am not even sure where to begin," Andy said.

"With the first step of course," came Sifu's response, quoting from a classic Chinese expression: "The journey of a thousand miles begins with the first step." Andy's martial arts brothers smiled at the reference.

"Okay. Let's begin with the Ni Zan painting because it is the first step you directed me to take. First, I went to see General Huang in Beijing. He was, to say the least, pleased to see his student's student. He told me you had written him more than a year ago about my visit—how is it that you knew this would happen?" Andy asked.

"It was one of many possibilities. But I am pleased that the two of you met. Go on," Sifu encouraged.

"I did your form for him in an impromptu exhibition and he yelled out that the opening was his own." Andy then told of the entire afternoon, including the "breaking the wrong brick" story, which made Sifu roar with laughter and exclaim, "So who taught you showmanship?"

Andy continued, "General Huang was wonderful. He reminisced about your uncle and your father and the warlord period of the 1920s. He still remembers it clearly. He gave me a piece of his own calligraphy and a book about Beijing in the 1920s and 30s. The gifts were very unexpected. His daughter embarrassed me when she gave me these gifts because I had nothing to give in return," Andy added quietly, looking at Sifu.

"You underestimate the value of his seeing traditions preserved, of having his contributions honored," said Sifu.

"He's the oldest living general in China," remarked Dr. Yip, "but he is forgotten by many. You made him alive and relevant in front of his troops—when they see him again, they will remember too."

"His daughter will prove to be a great ally for you in the future. She is a retired colonel from the People's Liberation Army," said Sifu.

"That would explain how she was able to find me so easily the next morning. I had moved to another hotel unexpectedly the night before, yet she was there the next morning. I was a bit surprised but did not think too much of it at the time. She said I was a little too famous—I thought she meant from my martial arts exhibition at the compound," Andy said.

"And this was the first time you were attacked?" Sifu confirmed.

Andy nodded, not surprised that Sifu knew all the details.

"See," Peter said to Sifu. "He's become a dangerous guy to hang out with."

"I also traced where the painting came from because I thought you'd be interested in the provenance. I mean, it's obviously the real thing, even Dr. Yip recognized it as such."

"He was probably there when Ni Zan painted it," offered Peter, sotto voce.

"Let's hear it," demanded Tommy.

"Well, it was in the Imperial Collection and then it was given as a gift to a member of the Bao family in Beijing. They were a family who had produced generations of successful and high-ranking scholar officials in the Qing dynasty government. The painting was considered something of a prized treasure for the family. It was confiscated in 1929, to be sold for hard currency. A number of things from the Bao family were seized then shipped from Shanghai to a dealer here in Hong Kong. The dealer still exists today, and the records show that Sifu's uncle was an agent in the sales."

Danny, usually so quiet, gasped softly, but they all looked surprised.

Sifu nodded, not really surprised. "Both my father and my uncle served a warlord," he noted.

"It gets worse," warned Andy. "Both your father and your

uncle were at the Bao home the day the art was taken, but I think your uncle kept some of the art for himself and sold it a few years later for his own profit."

The others exclaimed out loud—Andy hadn't shared this yet.

"This isn't that surprising either," said Sifu sadly. "My father never discussed the rift with his brother, but it was clear he thought my uncle, his brother, had brought shame on the family. But how did you uncover this?"

"I tracked the art dealer who conducted the sales. We dug around in the warehouse this morning and found the catalogue and ledgers. The English woman who kept the records noted that the agent was Chan Daimon."

"And you think she wrote the Cantonese pronunciation of Chan for Chen and Daimon for Dawen," guessed Dr. Yip. Andy nodded.

"Yes, Dawen was the agent with Wang Shenming, who was likely another soldier helping in the scheme. But some of the art did not sell, and was just returned to Dawen at a Hong Kong address. The Ni Zan is part of this latter group."

"You have done well, Andy. You know more about this painting than I do. My brother gave it to me last year for 'safekeeping' as he put it. I thought it rather strange at the time, but did not question it. I knew that my uncle sold art when he needed cash, but I never knew where the objects had come from."

"But there is more," added Andy quickly. "I've come across other pieces from the Bao family collection—some from a private collection in the US and one, a magnificent jar, sold to a colleague in Ocean Terminal."

"Yes, Peter told me about the jar," said Sifu, "but he didn't mention it was connected."

"I didn't know," protested Peter.

"It's on the same list, so I think it is," explained Andy.

"What list?" demanded Tommy, ever with an eye on the bottom line.

"The list of items taken from the Bao family," explained Andy.

"Did you find it in one of your books?" asked Danny quietly.

"No, no. I met a descendant of the Bao family here in Hong Kong." Andy turned back to Sifu. "Amazingly, he is the one I sought out to repair your painting."

"There are no…" offered Sifu.

"… coincidences," finished Andy. "This is another one of the streams joining the others. He said that a young man had brought it in a few years ago but had left in a hurry when Zheng suggested it was a stolen object."

"Did he get a name?" asked Peter.

"No, but I got the impression it was someone my age."

"Not my brother then," concluded Sifu, and then they all reached the next conclusion.

"Sifu," said Tommy. "We need to consider that your nephew had a role in recent events."

"Why did your brother give you the painting?" asked Andy.

"Yes, this is indeed an excellent question. But you're really asking if my brother gave me the tea, too. This is the very question we were discussing when you came in." Sifu paused to get back to where they had been in their discussion. "What we do know is that the Dragon Well tea, formerly located in my kitchen, had a toxin in it that was meant to poison me. My nephew gave me that tea as a New Year's gift earlier this year. The Ni Zan painting, however, came to me months before that. Indeed, my brother brought it by about a month before he died."

"But why would your nephew try to kill you?" asked Danny. "If he wanted the painting back, why not ask for it?"

"I'll have to ask him," said Sifu quietly.

Early the next morning, Andy met all his brothers in Victoria Park. Even Danny and Tommy had come over from Lantau Island. Sifu was still too weak to join them but he had given them something to work on the night before.

After warming up and doing several forms together, the four of them paired off to work on a combination of "pushing hands" and "sticking hands" exercises. Each pair faced each other in a bow stance, a three-quarter stance with one foot forward and slightly bent and the rear leg straight back. Moving forward and back, they both simultaneously rocked their hips in a kind of elongated figure-eight movement. The hand movement began rather simply and slowly. While one moved forward, he pressed the forearm of the other, which was held steady in front of the body. As the defender then became the attacker, the hands would shift; the one would stop the press and offer the forearm, while the other pressed both hands on his forearm.

After a short while the speed would pick up. The hands would start to make large circles clockwise then counterclockwise. After a time they would both switch their feet, and the foot that was in back moved forward. The touch and attack were in constant motion. Each was "listening" to the other's movements. After half an hour, they were all sweating from the work. The exercise Sifu had given was to learn to express the self in the movement, to try not to anticipate the opponent's movements but to just be in the moment.

As Sifu noted, "Once one is able to express the self, then one can become benevolent and self-less."

When they were done, Tommy asked Andy if he could shower and change at Andy's apartment. Andy agreed happily. When they were done, Andy offered Tommy a cup of American coffee. Tommy perched on a rotating stool at the kitchen counter and turned to face the living room. Andy's apartment was decorated with books—they lined the hallway and most of the living room walls. He had traditional Chinese paintings on one side of the entry hall and some in his bedroom, but little other art on display. Andy's business was sporadic and some years he did better than others. His apartment looked like a scholar's rooms to Tommy. Aside from the books, the living room had a large square table pushed against a wall. There was a chair on either side with a tray in the center. On the tray was an assortment of ink stones, small scholar's desk rocks, and other carved stones. He had another table to the side, more cluttered, with his laptop and printer.

As Tommy looked it over he felt affection for his little brother. He began saying, "Andy, I must caution you again to be very careful. I know you are going with Sifu today to visit Chen Ding. We all think Ding is a fool, but perhaps he is only lacking in family spirit. He has started in with a real estate syndicate, and you can't get in there with less than three million US."

"Are you in?" asked Andy.

"No," answered Tommy shortly. He realized he had been short and he expanded. "I don't do business with this group. I don't care for their methods and I don't want to know where their money comes from. I'd never get out if I put in as much as a dollar."

"Oh," said Andy, catching Tommy's reference to organized crime. "But how does Ding get this kind of money?"

"I don't know. But these guys play hard, which means that Ding has learned a new game. And it must be a very new game because even Ah Pun hasn't recognized any of the players—or their teams. I am just saying to be careful," Tommy said, as he picked up his bag and headed out of Andy's apartment.

* * * *

Andy left soon after, hopping the ferry to Kowloon and knocking on Itchy's door hours before normal opening. Itchy was there, as he had agreed to be the night before when Andy called.

"Not wasting time, are we?" asked Itchy.

"Fine, and how are you this morning?" retorted Andy.

"I'm not sure yet—mebbe you know how I'm doing."

"No, Itch, I'm not bringing bad news. Instead, I may have discovered where the jar came from, at least when it left China."

"Whaddya have?" Itchy asked, interested in spite of himself.

"Well, remember how I said it sounded like a pot listed in a book I found in Beijing?" prompted Andy.

"Yeah sure. The book had the paintings in it."

"Yes, well, I ran across another person familiar with the collection."

"Can he identify the jar by sight?"

"No, it left China in the late 1920s, well before his time. But he produced a detailed list compiled by the family, with even more details about the jar. I think it's worth another look."

"This guy of yours," said Itchy, "what kind of interest does he have in the jar?"

"None that I can see," said Andy, "save for a family's quest to answer some old questions. The good news," Andy continued quickly, "is that his list might establish provenance and how the jar left China—which means we can advertise the sale anywhere we want."

"Let's go take a look then," conceded Itchy.

They left the shop and walked through Ocean Terminal, turning into—much to Andy's surprise—Andy's tailor's shop.

Mr. Mao looked up from his sewing machine and smiled a greeting at Andy.

"Back so soon, Mistah Andy. What can I do this time?"

Andy bowed. "This time, I am just with him." He nodded to Itchy, who stepped in behind Andy.

"Ah yes, Mistah Itchy's custom job. Let's go to back."

Itchy and Andy ducked under the dark curtain that separated the workroom from the sales area. Mr. Mao opened a closet door in the back and Andy was surprised to see a huge walk-in safe at the back.

"Used to be a jeweler's," confided Mr. Mao, "and it was too expensive to pull this one out." He swung the heavy safe door out and Andy saw that the trunk took up most of the space.

"It's a dandy hiding spot," admired Andy.

He and Itchy struggled to lug the heavy box out to the open work space. Huffing by the end, Itchy finally propped open the lid. Andy rummaged through his bag and pulled out the folio.

"See here." He pointed to the entry for Itchy to see.

Itchy pulled out his glasses and took the folio. "I can't read this. It's in Chinese."

"Right. Of course. Sorry." Andy took the pages back.

"Here, it says red and white porcelain jar." He paused while they both looked down.

"Check," said Andy. "Now, the next line: approximately twenty-four *zhi* high. One *zhi* is roughly an inch," he noted.

Mr. Mao produced a measuring tape and got down to measure from the base on up. Andy sat on the floor, cross-legged, next to Mr. Mao. Mr. Mao nodded. "Mouth approximately seven *zhi* in width."

Andy gingerly removed the lid and Mr. Mao measured the opening. Again, he nodded.

"'Nine registers of decoration: three of scrolling flowers, one of cloud thunder pattern, two of lotus petals, two of Persian arabesque, and one large central register of auspicious plants,'" Andy read.

As Andy listed each attribute, Mr. Mao pointed them out to Itchy.

"Yes," said Andy, running his fingers down the jar, "this *yunleiwen* pattern, the cloud and thunder pattern, derives from ancient Chinese bronze decorations. The rest of these are a wonderful combination of Chinese and Persian decoration, as we would expect of a jar from the fourteenth century."

Itchy peered over his glasses and then he nodded. "It's not my area, but I think I am with you so far."

Andy continued translating, "'No glaze on the bottom—no kiln marks.'"

Mr. Mao looked alarmed.

Andy reassured him, "We've already checked."

Mr. Mao looked relieved that they would not be lifting the heavy pot.

"Is there anything about the lid?" asked Itchy.

"Yes," confirmed Andy. "And this should be the clincher, I think. Let's see. 'Three bands of decoration, one of lotus pattern, one of Persian arabesque and one of scrolling peonies, with solid red finial.'"

"Ahhhh," said Andy in quiet satisfaction. The lid indeed matched this description.

"So, that's that," said Itchy.

"Yes, this must be the same pot," agreed Andy. "This is actually more than usual, to go on I mean. Often a written description or catalogue entry is sparsely detailed. Even so, the lid is so distinctive that no one can have any doubts."

The three men contemplated the jar for a moment. Andy broke the silence.

"Let's put it back now." He swung the chest around and was surprised to see a familiar logo on the upper left side. On a faded sticker, the kind usually found on steamer trunks, Andy recognized the stylized Han dynasty dragon of Hong Kong Arts. Andy let out another breath.

"Anything wrong?" inquired Itchy.

"No, just another stream joining the river," he acknowledged ruefully.

Itchy peered over his glasses again, but Andy wasn't visibly distressed, just quietly going nutty. He snapped the trunk shut, breaking Andy's reverie.

"Let's lock it back up again," suggested Andy.

* * * *

Andy took the ferry back to the Hong Kong side and made his way to Dr. Yip's. Ah Pun leaned against Tommy's car by the front door. They nodded at each other. Andy buzzed and waited for Sifu to come down. Andy was not surprised that Sifu managed without assistance.

"I'm over it," said Sifu, referring to the constant care and scrutiny.

"My mother would say you're fine if you're able to complain," noted Andy.

"No fool, she," replied Sifu. They all got into the car.

Chen Ding's office was located in Happy Valley. It was on the second floor of a new tower overlooking the Hong Kong Jockey Club, in a building either sleek and modern or unimaginative and sterile. Ah Pun, who had parked and joined them, just snorted. He had preceded them in, glanced about, then held the door for Sifu and Andy to enter after he deemed it safe. Sifu walked up to the receptionist and gave his name, asking to see Chen Ding. He acknowledged he didn't have an appointment but that Mr. Chen would consent to fit him in. Sifu smiled gently at her, and the receptionist disappeared through the door. Moments later, Chen Ding burst through and bowed awkwardly to Sifu.

"Uncle, what an honor. How are you feeling? You look much recovered." His voice trailed off under Sifu's gaze. Sifu just waited. "Oh, yes, yes, do not stand there, come in and sit down." He led Sifu through the doorway. Andy and Ah Pun he ignored entirely, but they trailed behind, undaunted.

He led Sifu into another severely appointed office with a chrome and glass table, a chrome and glass desk, mostly empty, and a metal sideboard. Sifu sat in a chrome and leather chair. He had yet to say anything to Ding.

"Have you been home yet? I've been watering your plants for you. The apartment is fine," Ding said nervously.

Andy opened his mouth to speak but Ah Pun's grin quieted him again. Ding babbled on, ill at ease and unable to stop speaking. "Let me get you something. Would you like something to drink? Or to eat?"

"I'm here, dear nephew, to talk to you about tea," Sifu said quietly.

"Tea?! Why does everyone want to talk about tea?!" demanded Ding petulantly, notwithstanding thousands of years of culture. Sifu raised his eyebrows. Ding rushed to explain.

"You should speak to my partners. They aren't here now, but they also like to talk about tea. They try to interest me, too."

"Really?" encouraged Sifu.

"Yes, oh yes. They asked me once if I liked tea—I don't care about it but I wanted to be pleasant. I remembered the kind at my father's house, so I told them I liked Dragon's Well tea and jasmine tea. Then they had to go and give me some and I couldn't refuse but really I wasn't going to drink it. Actually, I gave some to my father."

"He didn't drink Dragon's Well tea, nephew."

"He said he liked to have it in the house," came the quick response.

A shadow passed over Sifu's face as he realized his brother kept it in case Sifu came by, despite the rift between them.

"Anyway," continued Ding, "I didn't give it all to him. I gave you a canister, too."

"My tea was poisoned," said Sifu softly.

"Waaaaah?" Ding's voice trailed off and his mouth hung open. His shock was palpable and he turned paler than the unhealthy shade he usually sported.

Sifu looked at him in silence. Andy and Ah Pun barely moved. Andy looked away.

Sifu sighed. "My nephew," he said, quietly but in command, "we are not close but we are all the family that is left. You will tell me now what is going on."

"Nothing, Uncle, everything is fine," protested Ding weakly.

Sifu held up his hand and Ding subsided.

"You will tell me today," instructed Sifu, and he settled back into the ungodly uncomfortable chair. "You will explain why you are afraid," continued Sifu.

"I'm not afraid," protested Ding, "but it is possible that my partners want to kill me."

Andy and Ah Pun's eyes met. Get in line, they both thought. Sifu flicked them a glance and they assumed neutral expressions again.

"Did you know about the poison?" asked Sifu.

"No, I had no idea. I'd never give it to family if I thought it dangerous. Aiyaah, do you think it killed my father?" Ding's face crumpled into misery.

"It is possible, especially if he drank it when the poison was fresher," Sifu explained.

"My father knew these people, but he warned me against them. I did not see any harm," admitted Ding.

"What is happening now?" Sifu prompted.

"I am having trouble raising my share for the real estate syndicate. I joined because I had the initial sum, but then they demanded another million. I did not have it and I told them so."

"How did they react?"

Ding flushed with embarrassment. "They threatened me here and then came into my house a few weeks back. I was afraid." He hung his head in shame.

"Nephew, you are holding yourself stiffly I see, more so than just being in my presence deserves. Did they hurt you?" asked Sifu gently.

"Yes," admitted Ding softly. "I didn't know how to stop them, so I finally offered my father's prized possession, an antique jar. I found it after he died, but he had told me that there was a piece he had held on to if we ever needed it, one that was worth over a million dollars. But he didn't want to sell it."

"A red and white ceramic jar? . . . a big one? . . . one with a lid?" asked Andy.

"Not really red, more grey and white," said Ding, annoyed at Andy's interruption and thinking to correct the foreigner.

"Why didn't he want to sell it?" asked Sifu.

"I don't know. I think he had recently sold a painting. It was gone anyway when I looked for it, and I looked everywhere. As he got older, he developed an odd sensibility about the art his own uncle had left to him. But I don't think he liked my partners."

"Did he say why?" probed Sifu.

"Not really. He seemed to know one of them from a long time ago and was uneasy. He didn't explain why, and he died a few months later."

"Why didn't you go to the police?" asked Sifu.

"And tell them what? It wasn't the kind of deal that had paperwork, and I had no proof. If the police poked around, my partners would just return and I'd end up broke or dead."

Andy wondered briefly which fate Ding dreaded more.

Sifu bowed his head for a moment. Then he looked up.

"Nephew, how do I contact these men?"

"I have a telephone number," Ding offered, "but what are you going to do?"

"End this, young nephew."

* * * *

The three men were quiet when they returned to the car, which was normal for two of them, but not for Andy.

"Let's talk with the others," Sifu said at last. "Ah Pun, I am sorry to create extra work for you, but after you drop us back at Dr. Yip's, please pick up the big jar from Mr. Itchy. Andy can make those arrangements. And please return and collect my nephew. He will need some things for a few days away from the office. You'll need to bring him by Dr. Yip's, too, so that someone looks at his injuries."

Ah Pun nodded.

"And take his mobile phone away."

Ah Pun grinned.

"I need to speak to Tommy and then to Peter," sighed Sifu. Andy pulled out his mobile phone and offered it to Sifu. Sifu stared at it a moment.

"I dated a woman once who thought mobile phones exemplified what is wrong with the modern world," offered Andy next.

"The loss of peace and privacy?" ventured Sifu, as he gingerly took the mobile unit.

"No, the immediate gratification thing," Andy answered. Sifu nodded in understanding, perhaps sympathy.

"She also really hated plug-in air fresheners," said Andy. Now Ah Pun and Sifu stared at Andy.

"You know," explained Andy, "those things that look like little night-lights, and you plug them in, and they let off artificial scent in the room."

"Why do you plug it in?" asked Ah Pun. Ah Pun rarely spoke when he drove, but some things had to be explained.

"That's just it," agreed Andy. "It's an American thing, to squander energy because they have so many energy sources—to drive huge cars or put two dishwashers in a kitchen. And now, a mini-appliance to keep the room smelling like summer breezes."

"Like mildew?" asked the Hong Kong native, totally at sea now.

"No, no, it's a marketing thing in America, to make a wholesome and fresh scent," explained Andy.

"Americans are very clean, in a determined way," commented Sifu.

"Yes, they are sanitized for their own protection," agreed Andy. "But back to the present. Sifu, just press three and it will speed dial Tommy."

"Okay. I will ask Tommy to track down the names of Ding's real estate partners and find out where they can be found. And let's see if Peter can track these telephone numbers that Ding gave us—if it's the same group."

"We didn't ask Ding for their names, but I'll bet one of them is the Mr. Wong that found Itchy," offered Andy.

"Yes," said Sifu, as he dialed the first of the numbers. "But first let's let Dr. Yip know we'll be home in time for lunch."

* * * *

It was only early afternoon, and indeed lunchtime, when they arrived back at Dr. Yip's. They opened the door to heavenly smells. Peter had made himself at home in Dr. Yip's kitchen and there were steaming bowls of noodles mixed with delicate fish, bok choy, and scallions in a savory broth.

"It turns out," said Sifu at last, to the full group that had assembled for lunch, "that my own thrifty nephew poisoned me."

The others looked up from their bowls.

"Why would he want you dead?" asked Danny somberly.

"He didn't," answered Sifu. "He only wanted to give me some tea that he did not want for himself."

"Did he give tea to anyone else?" asked Dr. Yip, concerned for other patients.

"Possibly his father, but no one else," answered Sifu.

"Not the same tea?" asked Yip, horrified.

"Not the same tin, but other ones were likely tampered with."

"Is it a sick joke?" asked Danny.

"No, but it appears that my nephew was the target. He was given the tea by his own business partners," replied Sifu.

"It's true that he isn't well liked in the business," noted Tommy, "but that alone isn't reason to kill him. These partners are men more likely to do something only if it is necessary to the business plan. But it could be as simple as wanting Ding to shut up about something."

"It's possible that his partners simply didn't have any further use for him," offered Danny.

"Then you are not the targeted victim, Sifu, which is a great relief," said Peter.

"Yes, in some ways. But I am responsible for my nephew and so it remains my problem."

"What shall we do next?" asked Andy.

"Let's find out who we are dealing with first," said Peter. "I'll start with the telephone numbers." He got up and pulled on his jacket. "I'll call when I know more."

"I, too, am returning to my office," said Tommy. "Let me make some calls and get some names."

Andy remained behind in the room, staring at the wall. Sifu looked at him until he became aware of the other's regard and unspoken question. "Do we give Ding back his porcelain jar, though the item itself carries no meaning to him?"

"First, we must address the problem of Ding's so-called business partners," responded Sifu.

"Since you are not involving the police, I assume you will let them drown themselves?" offered Dr. Yip.

"We don't have the kind of evidence that will interest the police, and it may be that my nephew's involvement will not bear up under police scrutiny." After a moment of thought, Sifu turned toward Dr. Yip and agreed, saying, "Yes, I think we should let them drown themselves."

"Are we throwing them into the harbor?" asked Andy, only half in jest, knowing that the other two were speaking in riddles and historical allusion. Both men gave Andy a quick glance then glanced at each other. Andy understood that, without words, they had just agreed to enlighten him.

"The reference comes from the collected works of Liu Zongyuan of the Tang dynasty," Dr. Yip explained, and Sifu nodded in agreement. "The story is known as 'The Man Who Liked Money Better than Life.' It goes something like this: In ancient times, there was a small town that had many good swimmers. One day, the river swelled suddenly. Braving the danger, about half a dozen people started across in a small boat, but while they were midstream, the boat capsized. They all started to swim. One, though using his arms vigorously, seemed to make small progress. 'You're a better swimmer than any of us, why are you lagging behind?' asked his companions. 'I have a thousand coins tied around my waist,' said the man. 'Why don't you throw them away?' urged the others. But he made no answer, shaking his head and clearly tiring quickly. The others reached the shore and shouted back to him: 'Off with the coins, you fool! What's the use of money to you when you are drowning?' Still, the man shook his head. A few moments later, he drowned."

"So how do we help Ding's partners to drown themselves?" asked Andy.

"It should not be too difficult," came Sifu's reply.

"I'll leave my door unlocked," noted Yip, as he took himself off to his study and left the men to wait.

* * * *

Tommy called in first. "I made several calls," he said, "and many colleagues had heard of the group, but mostly from Chen Ding. Ding called it New China Enterprises and claimed to be developing land on Lantau Island. The odd thing is, no one has met the partners. It's just Chen Ding dropping these names."

"What names did you hear?" asked Sifu.

"Just two names—Wong and Su," Tommy replied.

Sifu thanked him and broke the connection. He dialed his nephew's number and found Ding still in his office. He spoke to him quickly in Mandarin, listened, and hung up.

"My nephew says that Wong is the main partner. He says Wong is in charge but that he speaks more often to Su, who in turn answers only to Wong. Wong did take the time to visit Ding at his home the other night, overseeing the beating. He had both Su and two other men with him—it was the other men who administered the blows."

"I wonder if I met most of this group when we bought the jar. The agent called himself Mr. Su and he had two men—the muscle—with him. It was actually the second time we had seen the muscle men," said Andy.

"Yes. I had Ding give me the address used for New China Enterprises, at least on the initial business cards he got from Mr. Wong and Mr. Su. I'll call Peter and add that to our information."

* * * *

"The address doesn't exist," said Peter, calling back half an hour later. "It's not even close to anything with that postal code. The mobile phone numbers are registered to a Mason Li, who has a shop on Canton Road a block from Ocean Terminal."

"That's near Itchy's shop," said Andy in surprise.

"Looks like. Well, we had wondered how they picked Itchy. It looks like the shop was simply close by," said Tommy.

"The jar is large and heavy, especially in that trunk. It would have been a nuisance to lug it around," acknowledged Andy.

"The other two names, Wong and Su, don't show up in the fraud unit's computers, nor do they have criminal records—under those surnames, at least."

"What is it they really do?" asked Andy.

"Hong Kong offers many opportunities," said Peter.

"Let's drop in on Mr. Li," suggested Andy.

* * * *

Scarcely an hour later, Andy and Peter stood in front of the Canton Road address. "It's a ceramics business," said Andy in amazement. They stood in front of a shop barely one block from Itchy's. The window revealed shelves of jars, plates, platters, and figures, all in bright, colorful patterns, many with gold edges.

"And it's called New China Exports," noted Peter.

"New doesn't have to mean ugly," protested Andy, as he and Peter entered.

It was as cluttered inside as the window display outside, and many of the wares had a fine coat of dust. The shelves lined all the walls. Andy felt himself drawn to the section of blue and white designs, notably, the stylized blue dogs, with their huge tongues lolling and gilt all around the edges.

There were no attractive Chinese women in this shop to greet customers. A chubby clerk finally emerged from the back. "Hi there, are you Mister Li?" asked Andy in an overloud voice. His English sounded very American suddenly.

"I am Mr. Chang. May I help you?"

"I'd like to buy some of this blue and white pattern—do you ship to the US?"

"We ship anywhere, sir, but we only handle large orders," replied Mr. Chang.

"I can order big. I own a couple'a stores on the east coast of the US. You know, the United States. And I need just this kind of mer-chan-dize," said Andy drawing out the last word.

Peter hid a smile.

"But I want to deal with Mr. Li only," he repeated loudly.

An older Chinese man stepped out. He wore the ubiquitous three-piece suit of Hong Kong businessmen. "I am Mr. Li. How can I help you today?"

"I'm in the China business," said Andy. "My name is Andy

Panda and this is my associate Peter Loo—he'll translate if you can't keep up with my English."

Peter bowed slightly, happy to hide his grin.

"Mister, aah, Panda," said Mr. Li gently, because one must speak gently with foreign idiots, "this is not a convenient time for us. Perhaps I can recommend another shop for you to try?"

"No, no, I'll be quick. At first I thought I liked this blue and white, but now that I think about it, I'm really interested in red and white." Mr. Li looked puzzled and tried to interrupt, but Mr. Panda could not be stopped. "I like large red and white pieces, like maybe a big jar, one with a lid mind you. And it'd have to come in a nice box... for transportation. Everyone likes a nice box, don'cha think, Mr. Li?"

Mr. Li's eyes narrowed and he looked more closely at Mr. Panda, noticing the Hong Kong tailoring and styling of his clothes.

"I have a friend, Mr. Li, who says your shop—well, at least your boss Mr. Wong—sold him a huge red and white jar recently. I'd like another one just like it."

"There is no one here with those names," Li replied blandly, but Andy just got louder.

"I want to speak with him about a big red and white jar and it's important. Just tell them to call me. I need to find them and I will—I got this far, didn't I? You just have them call me—tell that Mr. Su to stop counting his money for just a second so we can talk. Here's my card."

Andy dropped his card in Mr. Li's hand and turned heel and out the door. Peter shrugged his shoulders and followed Andy before Mr. Li could respond.

* * * *

Andy and Peter went round to Itchy's shop to fill him in and suggest he close up early, just in case Mr. Su thought he could find

Andy Panda at Itchy's shop. Andy and Peter helped Itchy close up. "You really know how to win friends and influence people," noted Itchy.

"I try not to disappoint," agreed Andy.

Ah Pun was waiting in the loading zone of the Ocean Terminal garage. "The Turtle's Egg of a nephew is already at Dr. Yip's and the jar is in the trunk," Ah Pun said as he answered Andy and Peter's unasked questions. They all got into the car to head for Dr. Yip's apartment. Andy's cell rang as they pulled out of the garage and turned onto Salsbury Road and the Cross Harbour Tunnel.

"Hello," Andy answered, loud and American.

"Mr. Panda, you are not happy with your purchase?" asked an unfamiliar voice, speaking British English.

"It was stolen—taken just a few years ago from an excavation." Andy was making it up as he spoke. "I found reference to it in police reports while I was in Beijing."

"That is nonsense."

"No, it's on the watch list with the Hong Kong police, part of a list that is checked against the auction houses sales. That's why you couldn't sell it at auction here yourself," accused Andy.

"That jar left China in the 1930s, the spoils of a quarrel between old friends. None of the old friends will make a claim for it now," came the response.

"Well, okay, if we are telling the truth now, it comes down to this, Mr. Wong. It wasn't your jar to sell. It belonged to Mr. Chen, who was not ready to sell it yet," stated Andy.

"It wasn't Mr. Chen's to sell, Mr. Panda, any more than it was his father's to sell! Although his father did very well for many years on the proceeds of his trickery, it turns out he could not afford the interest payments when they came due," came the contemptuous response.

"What? What is that supposed to mean?" Andy asked.

"Please end this game. I know who you are. You have become a great annoyance to me. I have the right to sell the jar. You might say that Chen Ding had no right to sell the jar, that his family needed to pay a debt to mine."

Andy was astonished. This was a personal vendetta.

"Mr. Wong, why are you so interested in the wrongs done to the Bao family?" asked Andy, but Mr. Wong had hung up.

Andy's mind raced. Mr. Wong had taken up the Bao family's cause, and with a vengeance. Was he somehow connected to Zheng? Maybe Ding had started it all when he brought the Ni Zan into Zheng's shop. For all Andy knew, Ding had left his card or his full name when he went to the restorer's business. It would be easy enough to have found him after that.

Ah Pun pulled up in front of Dr. Yip's apartment. Andy and Peter lugged the chest up to Dr. Yip's back room. Ding got up when they entered but did not offer to help. He trailed along behind them.

"Hey, that's my trunk—where did you get it? Did you bring back my jar?" he demanded.

Sifu and Yip drifted in too.

"No," replied Andy. "We brought this here to protect the new owner from unwelcome attention in the next few days. This is likely to be as safe a spot as my tailor's shop."

"It's mine. I want it back."

"Your friend Mr. Wong didn't think it was yours to sell. He sounded like someone who is related to the Bao family, someone who was entitled to sell the jar as the rightful owner."

Ding snorted.

"Ding," asked Peter, "why didn't your father want you to work with Wong?"

"He said my great-uncle had had business dealings with him, many years ago, and that Wong was not to be trusted." Ding looked up at all the men watching him, and, uncomfortable, went back to the living room.

"Is he really the owner?" asked Peter quietly

"It's hard to say," admitted Andy. "It appears that it was stolen by his grandfather, and Ding might know or suspect it was stolen too, which is why he didn't try to sell it himself. It's hard to see his claim succeeding under the circumstances, especially against a member of the Bao family. And Itchy has a pretty good claim to it as a purchaser in good faith—we checked many sources to exclude the possibility that it was a stolen object. I think that Ding will be outta luck, and that it will be up to Itchy and the Bao family to sort it out, perhaps in court."

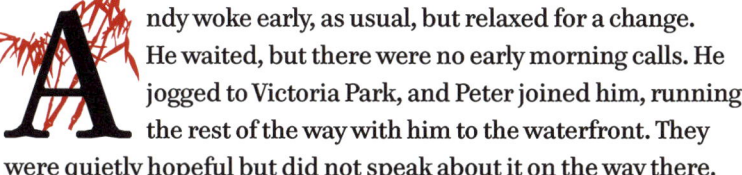ndy woke early, as usual, but relaxed for a change. He waited, but there were no early morning calls. He jogged to Victoria Park, and Peter joined him, running the rest of the way with him to the waterfront. They were quietly hopeful but did not speak about it on the way there.

At Victoria Park they went to the Pavilion.

Andy let out a deep breath when he recognized Sifu sitting on a nearby bench. Sifu smiled at them and said, "You are getting lazy without me. I've been waiting for half an hour."

Within minutes, they were joined by Tommy and Danny, who had anticipated the same event. Sifu began some breathing and qigong exercises with them, saying, "Remember, 'the mind commands, strength goes along, and internal energy follows.'"

This was a phrase all four had heard many times and they began to focus on the words and their meaning. Without thinking, all four students began to follow their teacher's movements and breathing patterns. This was Sifu's method of introducing a lesson. He wanted them all to be united in body, mind, and spirit, both relaxed and focused on the lecture and the movement to come. Andy knew from experience that this was when Sifu decided what needed to be discussed or taught that day. He would get a feel for them, a sense of what was troubling them, either about the physical movement or an intellectual or spiritual question.

After twenty minutes, they were entirely relaxed. Sifu faced the small group, which fell into a loose semi-circle.

"I am reminded of a story," Sifu began. "There was a young boy who sought out a great martial arts master. He found one living in the mountains. Night and day, enduring rain and hot sun, he waited outside the humble cottage. Finally the master came out and said 'What do you want?' The young man begged, 'I want to be a great master like you! How long will it take to achieve that?' The master responded, 'Ten years!' The boy said, 'Ten years! What if I practice twice as hard every day?' The master said, 'Twenty years!' The boy said, 'Twenty years! What if I practice all day long without ever sleeping?' The master laughed and said, 'Thirty years!' Baffled, the boy said, 'How is it that the time taken increases the harder I work?' The master said, 'If you keep one eye always on the destination it is so much harder to see the road along the way.'"

When Sifu finished, he looked at the group for a moment without speaking. They all realized that was the end of the lesson. They bowed to him, saying, "Thank you for teaching us." With that, they all began to leave.

Peter started to walk away with Andy and asked, "That was quick. What was that about?"

Andy replied, "I don't know. But I am sure that it was directed at one of us, maybe all of us."

Peter added, "Maybe it was one of those lectures where we don't get it for another ten years."

"Maybe never." Andy laughed with Peter as they both walked back up the hill towards their respective apartments.

* * * *

After Andy returned home, he sat down at his desk and began to gather his notes and research about the Bao family collection and where the pieces had appeared over time. He was tempted to return to Mr. Zheng and confront him with his efforts to obtain his family's legacy. Andy glanced over his notes from the warehouse, and his eye caught on a now-familiar family name—Wang Shenming. It was the name listed with Chen Dawen as agent for the sale of the Bao family items through Hong Kong Arts. It was there all along, but Andy had never focused on the other name. And then there was that logo, which had remained unchanged since the founding of the company, and which Andy found on the outside of the trunk.

This was the link—just as Chan and Chen are alternate spellings of the same name, Wang and Wong were alternate spellings of a common family name. The personal element in Wong's dealings derived from business dealings more than eighty years ago. Wong had targeted Sifu's family, the Chens, deliberately. Chen Ding was not the target per se, nor his father. It was the objects from the Bao collection themselves. When Chen Dawen had arranged to have the unsold items returned to a Hong Kong address and not to the business he and Wong Shenming had set up in Shanghai, Wong had been cheated out of the profits. And it looked like Chen Dawen had kept the art for himself and his own family, never compensating Wong in any way.

The current Mr. Wong, most likely the son of Wong Shenming, had somehow tracked down Sifu's brother and his foolish son Ding. Wong wanted more than the jar—he wanted revenge for a wrong done to his father all those years before. Sifu's brother had recognized the name and stayed away from Wong, but with him gone, Chen Ding had been easily manipulated.

Andy packed up in a hurry and left for Dr. Yip's apartment. He was eager to share his findings with Sifu and the others.

* * * *

As was his custom, Andy bounded up the stairs silently, bouncing on the balls of his feet. He burst through the door, catapulting himself into the arms of the two "muscles" he had met at Itchy's shop. On the other side of the room were the two who attacked Andy and Peter in the street. They had their guns drawn. Sifu and Dr. Yip sat on the small sofa in the living room. It was hard to say who was more surprised at Andy's sudden entrance—the two guards at the door could not react quickly enough to catch Andy as he bounded in. Andy recovered quickly and walked calmly into the living room. He pretended the men with guns were invisible, though he gave them wide berth, and started talking directly to Sifu.

"I figured something out and I wanted to talk to you right away."

"You couldn't call first?" asked Dr. Yip wryly.

"You again," stated one of the men with a gun. Andy recognized the two armed men as the ones who had attacked him and Peter in the street. The one speaking had worn the cheap leather jacket. "Just shut up and sit down."

"I can do that," Andy agreed, walking past him. "Nice jacket," he added, unable to resist.

Mr. Leather Jacket started to speak, but loud voices erupted from the back room. It must be Ding and Wong, Andy thought. The thugs looked back down the hallway.

"Do you mind if I make some tea?" asked Dr. Yip. He started to stand while Mr. Leather Jacket was still deciding whether he was needed down the hall. Clearly, the ancient Dr. Yip was the least of Mr. Leather Jacket's concerns, and he glanced back into the room at Yip. Not bothering to answer, Leather Jacket took a step forward and reached out his hand to shove Yip back into his seat.

Dr. Yip grabbed the outstretched hand with his own left hand, pulling it seemingly gently toward his own chest. This tiny man summoned huge strength, twisting Leather Jacket's hand effortlessly then stepping out of the way when Leather Jacket's momentum sent him hurdling past. Yip's right hand was free to grab Leather Jacket's gun while the bigger man was off balance, and Yip tossed it over to Andy.

No one noticed that Sifu had launched himself off the couch a beat behind Yip, landing once on the floor and springing up again to land again right in front of the second gunman. Sifu tapped him on the forehead and the gunman slumped to the floor. Sifu picked up the gun and emptied the chambers. He then handed that gun to Andy.

Dr. Yip, looking satisfied, said, "One should never attack a tiger with bare hands..."

"...nor cross a river without a boat." Sifu finished the saying. Both men looked at each other and grinned.

The guards at the door were practical street thugs, local boys who knew when to quit. They hadn't made a move to help the gunmen, nor did they threaten now. Sifu bowed to them slightly. They nodded their heads and slipped out the front door.

"Why did you let them go?" asked Andy, as he dragged the unconscious gunman into the living room.

"We do not need to make this too complicated," noted Sifu. "I'm sure Ah Pun can find them again if we need to."

Andy noticed that the noise had subsided from the back room. He started walking down the hall but stopped when he smelled the cigarette smoke. Chen Ding came stiffly down the hall, trying to muster some dignity, with Wong behind him. In back was Ah Pun, with his own gun in his hand.

"You need a better lock on the back door," he instructed Dr. Yip. "I phoned Peter already and the police are on their way."

Shenming Wong's son sat at the mahjong table, folding his arms in front of him. He had nothing left to say.

"I think I'll make that tea now," noted Dr. Yip.

* * * *

Hours later, the brothers had assembled around Dr. Yip's table along with Dr. Yip and Sifu. Ah Pun had melted away earlier through the back door when the police had pulled up in front.

"How did Wong find you?" asked Tommy.

"My nephew called him to demand half the sale price from the jar. It seems that Wong refused and my nephew told him that he had the jar back in his custody and would sell it himself."

"I thought Ah Pun took his mobile phone," protested Danny.

"He used the landline," explained Sifu.

"Some people do," commented Yip.

"Wong had caller ID and saw the number—it wasn't that hard to locate the address," explained Peter.

"What will happen to Ding?" asked Sifu. Ding had been taken by the police along with Wong and the gunmen. Peter had gone, too, while some of it was sorted out.

"It doesn't look like he did anything criminal—stupid, yes, but criminal, no," answered Peter.

"Are we even sure that he knew the art was stolen?" asked Danny.

"The police are not considering the items to be stolen, at least with respect to the 1929 transactions," replied Peter. "And if Wong turns over the sale price to Ding, Ding isn't likely to press charges."

"So Wong gets nothing?"

"Not so fast. We can get him for his instant dislike of our little brother," noted Peter.

Andy shrugged. "There's no accounting for taste."

"My guess is that Wong thought Itchy was a legitimate businessman, one with the means to pay cash for the jar but one outside the Asian art market. Andy's involvement was not antici-pated," said Peter.

"How did he find out I worked with Itchy?" asked Andy.

"You gave your card to one of the goons," chided Peter.

"It was the polite thing to do at the time," Andy defended himself.

The others smiled.

"He recognized your name from Sifu's brother's funeral. You made an impression. Wang was there and noticed you. When he saw your card," explained Peter, "he connected you to the Chen family."

"Did he break into my apartment?" asked Andy.

"It's hard to say. He alluded to having you watched in Beijing, and it was certainly his thugs who came after us in the street," said Peter.

"His pal, Mr. Su, recognized the name Hong Kong Arts when I mentioned it, though he denied it at the time. Maybe that worried them more," offered Andy.

"He wouldn't want you to trace the jar or figure out the connections. That's for sure," added Tommy.

"I regret, Andy, that my nephew is likely at fault for the apartment break-in. I suspect he entered my apartment to search for the Ni Zan painting. He ran into you instead with your full gym bag. When the Ni Zan wasn't at my apartment, he moved on to yours."

"Did he tell you this?" asked Yip sadly.

"Not in so many words," replied Sifu.

"It seems like a long way to go for Wong to exact revenge," noted Tommy.

"Maybe he just stumbled over Chen Ding and the opportunity presented itself," said Danny.

week later, Sifu had moved back to Lantau. Andy had finished writing up the catalogues for Preston's upcoming auction with a wonderful introduction on Ambassador Brookes' adventures collecting in the 1920s and 30s. Andy had also finished the valuations and write-ups for Doug, and, as Andy had suggested, arranged for Yoshio to buy the Muromachi screen as soon as it was available.

It had also been a week since Andy had seen Itchy. As he entered Itchy's shop, Andy heard, "Hello my young friend. Did ya find any more stolen objects for me?"

"Every day I see stolen objects, Itch."

"Yeah, well, it was new for me. It seems safer to stick with medieval stock."

"Because all the potential heirs are dead?"

"Something like that."

"The Bao family has no interest in asserting a claim to the jar, not after we told them that the Yamamoto Museum in Japan was interested."

"It's a big time museum, that's for sure."

"It's not really in Chen Ding's interest to make a claim either. His behavior in the past month was, er, erratic."

"That boy is plain stupid," Itchy said.

"No kidding. But he's not so stupid to refuse the compensation you offered to settle the matter."

Itchy nodded. The Yamamoto Museum offered five million US for the jar, as a quick resale without waiting for an auction. Andy collected his ten percent for his part in the deal, and Itchy paid another half a million to Ding.

"I'm sorry I ruined your triumphal return to Asia Week next spring."

"I'm going anyway—I'm writing a catalogue for one of the smaller auction houses and I want to be there for the sales. I'm sure the story will have made the rounds by then and I'll be famous at cocktail parties."

* * * *

Andy took the ferry back to Central. It was a lovely day and he looked forward to his next appointment. First he stopped by his apartment, where he was to meet Sifu. Sifu was there already, leaning against one of the chairs in the lobby waiting area and shaking hands with Pallas Athene. They were clearly finishing up a conversation, and she walked away to the elevators as Andy approached, nodding to him only.

"Do you know her?" Andy asked Sifu in amazement.

"What's wrong with speaking to a lovely women?" asked Sifu, not quite answering his question. "Come on, let's go," Sifu said, putting a hand on Andy's shoulder and pulling him along out of the building.

They took a cab to Queens Road West, where Andy rang the bell at Zheng Lin's shop.

They were buzzed in and once again Andy smelled sandalwood. Mr. Lin arrived quietly in the entry hall. He and Andy bowed to each other.

"It is a pleasure to see you again, my young friend," acknowledged Lin.

"The pleasure and honor are all mine. I have brought my Sifu, who is interested in your work."

"You would like to see your painting perhaps?" said Lin, as he led them into the work room.

"My student has told me of your life's work, Mr. Lin, and your ongoing tribute to your family's honor."

Mr. Lin paused at the compliment. He turned and noted, "I think we'll need tea."

Andy and Sifu followed Lin upstairs, to a solarium on top of the building. Andy had not seen this part yet, and he understood that Lin had decided that this was not a business meeting anymore. Comfortable benches lined the walls of the small bright room, and they sat. A young woman served tea and departed. The three men sat in silence for a few minutes, enjoying the moment and savoring the excellent tea.

"My family did not fit into the new China of the 1920s, Mr. Chen, but you bear no responsibility for what happened."

"And yet, as you yourself pointed out, the Ni Zan painting keeps coming home to you," offered Sifu.

"I just need to finish the story," protested Lin.

"I need to finish it, too," said Sifu quietly. "My own father tried to save the painting and my own brother wanted to save it in his own way. It is time for the story to end, now that the painting is home."

"I cannot accept this gift," Lin protested again.

"I cannot keep it for you any longer," stated Sifu.

Andy sat quietly for once, watching the two honorable men sort out the mess.

Lin tapped his finger against his teacup. He stood finally and said he'd return in a moment. Andy took the time to look closely at

Sifu, who was perfectly at rest in this quiet space. He noted that Sifu looked quite well, far less worn than he had been recently.

Sifu decided to notice Andy's scrutiny, asking, "Do you have something to say?"

For once, Andy just shrugged. Sifu feigned shock.

Lin returned with a large painting, rolled up and carefully tied. He slipped it into its silk wrapping.

"I will accept your gift, Mr. Chen. The Ni Zan has a special place in my family. In return, you must take this symbol of our gratitude, along with the blessings of the Bao family."

Sifu stood up and bowed. Andy could see that Sifu would permit this dignified end.

* * * *

"Let's stop by Yip's before we head to Lantau," said Sifu. "He has some foul tea for me to take home."

Andy smiled.

Yip welcomed them, as always. He made a foul brew indeed for Sifu and a gentler one for Andy.

"What's in the silk?" asked Andy. From nowhere, Yip produced a picture hanger.

Sifu gently unwrapped the painting and looped the hanger around the mounting. He slowly unrolled the painting, revealing the Lin Liang painting Andy had seen previously at Zheng Lin's shop.

"A magnificent painting," approved Yip.

"Very much to my taste—in some ways, more than the Ni Zan," noted Sifu.

"Sifu, did you know where the Ni Zan came from?" asked Andy.

"I knew some of the history, but not all of it. I didn't know about the Bao family connection. I did know that you could sort it out," Sifu replied.

"Because I know about paintings," said Andy.

"Yes, but also because you let your emotions guide you, and they let you make intuitive leaps and find connections that were long hidden."

"But you tell me I am hasty and impetuous," replied Andy.

"Sometimes it's a good thing," explained Yip, who rarely explained. "A week ago, you burst into this apartment, excited by your discoveries, sailed past two muscle men, and sassed the really bad guy with a gun. Your energy changed the dynamic and distracted our guards. You changed the balance of a most unpleasant encounter."

Sifu smiled. Andy shrugged, then grinned back.

"Now then, I hear you'll be marrying Peter's niece," continued Dr. Yip. Andy fled.

* * * *

Andy returned to his building, nodding as always to Wong Hei. He entered the elevator and pushed the button to his floor.

"Hold the door!"

Andy heard a woman's voice and pushed the door open button. Pallas Athene hurried in.

Andy took a deep breath.

"Hi," he said, holding out his hand, "I'm one of your neighbors. My name is Andy Boyd."

"Rachel Kincaid," she replied, shaking his hand. "And I know who you are. Chen Xiaohu recommended you highly."

Andy blushed, from the top of his head to the bottoms of his feet.